Robert Charles Jenkins

Alfonso Petrucci, Cardinal and Conspirator

An Historical Tragedy in Five Acts

Robert Charles Jenkins

Alfonso Petrucci, Cardinal and Conspirator
An Historical Tragedy in Five Acts

ISBN/EAN: 9783337182939

Printed in Europe, USA, Canada, Australia, Japan

Cover: Foto ©Andreas Hilbeck / pixelio.de

More available books at **www.hansebooks.com**

Robert Charles Jenkins

Alfonso Petrucci, Cardinal and Conspirator
An Historical Tragedy in Five Acts

ISBN/EAN: 9783337182939

Printed in Europe, USA, Canada, Australia, Japan

Cover: Foto ©Andreas Hilbeck / pixelio.de

More available books at **www.hansebooks.com**

ALFONSO PETRUCCI

CARDINAL AND CONSPIRATOR

AN HISTORICAL TRAGEDY IN FIVE ACTS

BY

ROBERT C. JENKINS, M.A.

RECTOR OF LYMINGE, HON. CANON OF CANTERBURY

LONDON

KEGAN PAUL, TRENCH & CO., 1, PATERNOSTER SQUARE

1882

TO THE RIGHT HONOURABLE

THE EARL GRANVILLE, K.G.,

LORD WARDEN OF THE CINQUE PORTS,
SECRETARY OF STATE FOR FOREIGN AFFAIRS,
ETC., ETC.,

THIS SKETCH OF THE CONTRAST BETWEEN

THE DIVIDED ITALY OF THE PAST

AND

THE UNITED ITALY OF THE PRESENT

IS INSCRIBED

WITH AFFECTIONATE RESPECT.

TO THE READER.

THE history of the Petrucci Conspiracy fills one of the saddest pages in the annals of the Roman Pontificate. It is described by Guicciardini in his thirteenth book, and in the biographies of Alfonso Petrucci, given by Palatius (*Fasti Cardinalium*) and by Eggs, in his *Purpura Docta*. The life of Leo X. which they give respectively in their "*Gesta Pontif. Romanorum*" and the "*Pontificium Doctum*" throws further light upon the melancholy narrative. The incidents of the conspiracy have been closely followed, the characters of Laodamia Petrucci and Violante Riario * being the only non-historic ones. They are designed to represent the spirit of the regenerated Italy of the present as contrasted with the demoralized Italy of the past.

* Laodamia was a name not unusual in the Patrician families of Tuscany. The sister of Pius II. was so named. Violante was the name of the mother of Riario.

DRAMATIS PERSONÆ.

PODE LEO X. (*at first, the Cardinal de' Medici*).
CARDINAL RIARIO,
CARDINAL SODERINI, } *involved in the conspiracy.*
CARDINAL SAULIO,
PANDOLFO PETRUCCI, *Lord of Siena.*
BORGHESE,
ALFONSO (CARDINAL), } *his sons.*
RAFFAELLO PETRUCCI, *Brother of Pandolfo.*
RINALDO PETRUCCI (*Father of Laodamia*), *Auditor of the Rota.*
THE ARCHBISHOP OF SIENA.
CARDINAL CORNELIO, *a friend of Alfonso.*
ANTONIO, *Secretary of Alfonso Petrucci.*
The Secretary of the city of Siena.
ORLANDO, *a Moor, formerly in the service of Pandolfo.*

LAODAMIA PETRUCCI, *Daughter of Rinaldo, engaged to Alfonso.*
VIOLANTE RIARIO, *Niece of Cardinal Riario, engaged to Borghese.*
THE DONNA MADDALENA, *Sister of Leo X.*

Citizens, Guards, etc.

The Scene alternates between the Palace of the Petrucci in Siena * and the Palace of the Vatican.

* The Palace of the Petrucci in Siena is said to have been founded in 1503 ; the promotion of Alfonso to the Cardinalate was in 1510.

ALFONSO PETRUCCI.

ACT I.

SCENE I.—*Siena. An Apartment in the Petrucci Palace.*
PANDOLFO PETRUCCI *and* CARDINAL RIARIO.

Pand. Lord Cardinal, thou hast been faithful found
Among the faithless. In that Court where reign
Intrigue and perfidy, yea, shameless guilt
And base forgetfulness of favours given
And faith reposed, thou still hast been the friend
True to my house and me ; and in this hour
Of my great need, the greatest and the last,
I seek thine aid anew.
    Ria.   What means my lord?
And how can I, well stricken now in years,
Feeble and faint, assist so great a prince?
    Pand. Thou know'st too well the history of my
        house—
How first it rose in pride of opulence
And lust of power o'er Siena's citizens,
Who hailed me as their father and their lord.

B

'Twas an inheritance that kings might envy,
That self-built throne—that tree of strength I planted.
Alas! the storm hath scattered to the winds
The hopes that erst like spring-tide leaves had clothed
My life ; and now the withered stem reveals
Its fourscore winters and their scathing rents,
And spring returns no more!

Ria.   And yet thine house,
While thou canst count such branches on thy stem
As Don Borghese and Alfonso, both
Of princely form and minds of grandest mould,
Might well defy the storms that shake the tree,
And only break the sapling.

Pand.   Would thy words
Were true as is thine heart!   Alas! Borghese
Affianced to thy niece, the fair Violante,
Seems to thine eye as once he seemed to mine,
Worthy to fill the place my death must soon
Make void.

Ria.   And doth thine heart proclaim him now
Unworthy thee—unworthy Violante?

Pand. I meant not that.   Right well I know that all
The warlike gifts, the high deserts which marked
Our race for glory, are in him renewed ;
Yet the fierce feud which gives dread prophecy
Of fratricidal guilt, of hands imbrued
In blood (O God!) from common sire derived,
Fills my last days with dreams of hideous guilt,
And my long nights with sleeplessness.

Ria.   Thy fears
How can I fail to share?   Our souls, alas!
In earlier day have drunk the maddening draught
Of wild revenge, and find, in vain remorse,

Its bitter after-taste ; and now we see
The poisoned cup passed on to those we love,
To drain even to the dregs—dread recompense
Of guilt yet unatoned.*

    Pand.   Oh ! mind me not
Of that foul deed ; I dare not scan the past,
When the grim future rises to appal me.
I know, ere yet from this spent frame the breath
Of life shall have gone forth, the younger son
Will claim the lordship which of right devolves
Upon the elder. Bold in plan and speech,
Fluent, persuasive, and unscrupulous
In all his course, Alfonso will appeal
To senate and to townsmen, bought and bribed
By promise fair of freedom, or by gold,
To give Borghese's heritage to him.
Could we but turn the stream of his ambition
Into some other channel—find some fount
Where he might slake the thirst for rule which burns
Within his soul !

    Ria.   Yet where could such be found
Save in some foreign Court, some warlike post
Where he might better even than here fulfil
His deadly hate—invoke some mightier power
Against Borghese's rule—with fire and sword
Bring desolation to these fruitful plains
Whose wealth he might not share ?

    Pand.   Such post would but

---

* Riario was involved in the conspiracy of the Pazzi against the
Medici, and Petrucci had caused the death of his father-in-law,
Niccolo Borghese (see Guicciardini, " Hist. d'Italia," c. iv.), and
is also believed to have caused, by poison, the death of Pope
Pius III. ("Eggs. Pontif. Doct.," p. 681).

Make the dread feud more fatal and inveterate.
Yet one resource is left. His soul's ambition
Needs to be fed—yea, sated—till it feels
No hunger save the hunger of despair
That nought remains to conquer. At the Court
Of Rome, amid the princely throng that fills
The stately Vatican, he yet may save
A proud name from dishonour, and a race
Born to command from baser destiny.

   Ria. And would you claim for him that cruel lot,
Which turns even friends to foes, and princes born
To cringing menials—a Cardinal's?
Is Rome more safe than Siena? Are no hands
Uplifted there to murder?

   Pand.   Yet what hand
Can part the brothers who may even this hour
Be stained with fratricide, save that which writes
Alfonso Cardinal—lifts up his soul
To higher life, his life to higher aims?
Oh, for her sake who soon will be the bride
Of him for whom I plead, I do entreat thee
To lay before his Holiness my prayer.
Disclose the fearful past—the future traced
In its grim light—and claim a father's love
For him who else may lose a father's name,
And write in anguish on his opening grave
That he dies childless.

   Ria.   But Laodamia!
Will she resign him? will he heed the voice
Even of the Pontiff, if his highest gift
Should sever him from her whose very soul
Hath linked its destiny of love with his?

   Pand. I cannot turn aside to gaze on those

Who may be near our path but must not cross it.
Alfonso, if he claim the higher life,
May well persuade the heart that claimed his love
To dedicate its bridal thoughts to heaven ;
And if he fail, her sire must be constrained,
By bribe of place or fear of our displeasure,
To make our cause his own.   Be this my part,
And thine our suit at Rome.
   Ria.   My task is light
To thine, and shall be well fulfilled.   This hour
I haste to Rome, and at the Pontiff's feet
Will raise thy prayer and mine.
   Pand.   'Tis well; I thank thee.
Thy love hath never failed me, and must now
Be doubly proved for Violante's sake.
Farewell ! God speed thy prayer !

Scene II.—*An apartment in the Petrucci Palace in
    Siena.*   Violante ; Laodamia.

  Viol. Our lives are one long mystery of grief:
A wayward fate at once unites and severs
Hearts that in faith are one.
   Laod.   And yet those hearts
Are schooled by this stern destiny to rise
To higher life.   'Tis ours to bind in one
Two kindred hearts, united once, now rent
Through mutual hate, still deepening, till the chasm
Of fratricidal guilt shall close on them,
To be their common tomb.   Oh, could we rise
Equal to such a work !
   Viol.   Yet have we striven

And toiled the lifelong day, as labourers sent
In earliest dawn to this sad labour-field ;
But we have prayed and watched and toiled in vain.
Each plea of love still makes their hatred deeper,
And fiercer their disdain.

  Laod.   Thy words are true ;
Yet what a circlet of uniting love,
But for one failing link, our souls might weld !
We love as sisters. Don Borghese's love
With thine is linked, and with Alfonso's mine.
But then the strongest link, the closest bond,
Is lost. In severance dread the brothers stand,
And the bright chain falls down on either side.

  Viol. Yet love, whose spell is stronger even than death,
May forge that missing link. It may be that
One work, one prayer is wanting ; * that one loss
May forfeit all our gain. We may not faint
While labouring for a heavenly crown like this.

  Laod. Thou hast well said. The missing link may fail
Even through that missing prayer. But hark ! the sounds
Of martial step, of voices pitched, methinks,
To height of altercation. Let us fall
Back to the distance, where yon dim recess
May hide us both.   [*They retire to the background.*

   Enter BORGHESE *and* ALFONSO.

  Alf. Whence this new frenzy ? Why these dagger looks,
Which like a papal curse glance forth to slay
Body and soul together ?

---

 * " Havendo (Dio) determinato il numero delle domande per le
quali la vuole concedere, una che sene lasci, non siamo esauditi."
—S. Caterina de' Ricci.

Borg.   Vile supplanter !
Thou smooth-faced Jacob, ready aye to steal
The birthright and the blessing ! Thinkest thou
That I have not unearthed thee ? brought to light
Thy base intrigues—thy bribes—thy canvassings
Of venal senators?
    Alf.   Thou dost misjudge me.
What have I got to bribe with ?   What my means
To force or to persuade ?   Thy hand hath snatched
From the last childhood of our aged sire
All that he had to give.
    Borg.   False tongue, thou liest.
All that I have he gave me as his heir ;
All that I hope for, but for thine intrigues,
Must soon be mine.
    Alf.   Such chance may Heaven forfend !
Is not all Siena wearied with thy guilt?
Hearest thou no curses muttered deep—no threats
Of vengeance struggling madly into life ?
And wouldst thou turn on me the tide of wrath
Which surges on and must engulf thee yet ?
Oh, worthy follower of the accursed Pazzi,
Twice   hath   thine hand   been   raised, like theirs, to
       shed
The blood of innocence.*   Behold these scars,
And dare, if dare thou canst, to deepen them.
                         [Uncovers his neck.
    Borg. Sayst thou this hand twice sought thy life ?
    Then draw.

---

   * "A Burghesio fratre suo ferro tentatus vulneris cicatrices ser-
vavit in gutture usque ad sepulcrum " (" Palat. Fasti Card.," tom. i.
p. 565).   This attempt to take his brother's life is said to have been
made twice (see Zedler, "Universal Lexicon," tom. xxvii. p. 1143).

May this third stroke be fatal.

> [*They draw.* Violante *and* Laodamia *rush to
> the front and stand between them, each holding
> the other's hands.*

Laod. Thy guardian angel and the saints that plead
For those they love have stayed thine hand.   Alfonso !
Forbear, if still thou lovest me.   If thy love
Is turned to hate, oh, let thy dagger first
Drink my heart's blood, ere yet a brother falls
Beneath thine hand.

Viol.   Borghese ! is the pledge
Thou gavest me false ?   Didst thou not promise me
Never to bear that weapon in thy breast
Which minded thee of guilt, and yet might tempt thee
To deed of murder?   Cast it, cast it from thee.
Live to repent, to love ; think of Alfonso
But as the husband of thy kinswoman,
The more than sister of thy Violante ;
And through this path may thy first love return.
Alas ! your looks are cold !

Borg.   The sight of thee
Hath chilled the fever-heat of wrath—disarmed
Awhile my firm resolve.

Viol.   Say not awhile,—
For ever.   Come, embrace him.

Laod.   Smile, Alfonso.
Look not so fearfully aside.   Come near ;
Embrace your brother.   Let the cause of God
Be for this once triumphant.   It will be
Your triumph, too ; a brighter crown than e'er
Your sire hath worn, or Siena yet can give !

> [*They embrace coldly, and retire on either side.*

Scene III.—*As before.* Rinaldo Petrucci ; Laodamia.

Rin. (*embracing* Laodamia). My daughter !
Laod. My sire, what brings thee hither ? Why should I
Dread most the presence that I most should love ?
Yet even the voices we most longed to hear
Seem burdened now with prophecies of grief.
Rin. Yet were it ill that loving voice should bear
False prophecy, or hide our coming fate.
The dangers that o'erhang our house and race
Thou know'st too well, I need not count them now.
Dark clouds, uprising from the distant past,
Brood o'er the future, and ere long must burst
In ruin o'er our heads.
    Laod.   What means my sire ?
    Rin. The unnatural feud which rends our race in
        twain
Must close its reign in blood, unless——
    Laod.   Oh, say—
What means that word *unless ?* Explain—interpret.
    Rin. Unless thy hand avert the fatal shaft,
Which else must pierce the souls of all we love.
    Laod. Oh, speak—what meanest thou ? How can *I*
        avert
A shaft I see not—know not whence it comes,
Or where its stroke may fall ?
    Rin.   Alfonso's life
Is in thy hands ; Borghese's fate is linked
With his, and ours with both.
    Laod.   I pray you speak
More plainly. Could I save Alfonso's life,

Mine own would be a willing sacrifice.
I would yield all for him—save his dear love !
   Rin. Yet that, and not thy life, must be the victim,
The one peace-offering.   Were his love for thee
As pure as thine—
   Laod.   Oh, doubt it not, my father !
   Rin. Yet must I doubt it, while ambition reigns
Supreme in all his life.   Ambition, child,
Is but a cruel stepmother to love.
His heart is proud of thee.   In thee he sees
One worthy of himself ; yet only worthy
Because thy mind, thy power, thy skill to win
The world he seeks to gain, will all be his—
His to supply the greed of his ambition,
Not slake the thirst of love.
   Laod.   Thou dost misjudge him.
How canst thou know Alfonso as I know him,
Who read his inmost thoughts ?   Alas ! too well
I read the tale of vengeance long suppressed,
Of pride indomitable, high ambition ;
And yet in every line a mystic truth
O'errules the literal sense.   That truth is love—
Love that presides o'er all his inmost thoughts ;
Love that even now hath made him sheathe the dagger
In bitter hatred drawn.   Oh, loving father,
Thou know'st but half his soul.
   Rin.   Yet say, my daughter,
Were he a murderer, could you love him still ?
   Laod. My love would save him from so dire a guilt.
   Rin. Yet if one only act of love could save,
Say, wouldst thou dare to do it ?
   Laod.   Cheerfully.
   Rin. And if that act cut off thy last fond hope,

Even as the offering of the patriarch,
And left thee lone in this world's wilderness——
    Laod. Oh, whither wouldst thou lead my darkening
       steps?
I cannot follow thee.
    Rin.   Suppose, then, that
Alfonso, called to higher state of life,
Were placed beyond the sphere of woman's love,
Except such love as springs from sacred tie
Of sister or of friend.   Couldst thou resign
The dearer name of wife and call thyself
The sister—guardian of his higher life
And heavenly destiny?
    Laod.   What higher life
Were mine on earth than his unchanging love?
Heaven hath for me no higher gift than this.
    Rin. Yet hath it higher gift for him.
    Laod.   What mean'st thou?
    Rin. In Rome 'tis said that in the next promotion
To the high dignity of Cardinal,
Alfonso's name in foremost rank will stand.
If this be so, wouldst thou surrender him——
Renounce thy claim as his affianced one—
Consent to be his sister, friend, and guide?
    Laod. Thou askest a hard thing; for could I see him
Raised like the Prophet to angelic state—
Unlike that great successor who discerned
His parting guide, and by that sight was raised
To claim a yet more wondrous ministry,
A doubled gift—mine eye would pale and fade,
My mission close, my life's work end for ever!
    Rin. Yet were his life to fall beneath the stroke
Of unmasked guilt or secret treachery,

As fall it must unless this deadly feud
For ever cease—what good would thy life do thee?
   Laod. Might not my love with gentlest hand arrest
The arm of guilt?   Might not the tender words
Of wife be as a spell to charm away
The darkest thoughts of vengeance, plans of guilt?
May not this be my lot, and were it well
That I should shrink from it?
    Rin.   I ask thee not
To yield thy love, but rather to exalt it
With his to higher state—to make it now
The handmaid of his soul along that path
Where all is peace.   As prince of Holy Church,
From that proud eminence he might look down
On the wild fray that makes our Tuscan plains
But an Aceldama, a field of blood ;
Bind up the wounds of our loved Italy,
Fallen among thieves, despoiled of all but life.
   Laod. Oh, could I read his future as thou read'st it,
And feel that peace could ever reign where reigns
Eternal warfare, and could reign through him,
I well might pray that in the Court of Rome
Alfonso's life might find a place of rest,
My lifelong love a grave.   Yet wherefore trust
To rumours wild as this ?   How know'st thou that
The Pope designs to raise him to the purple ?
   Rin. Here in my hands I hold the papal brief
Declaring him a Cardinal and commanding
His presence at the Court.
   Laod.   And deem'st thou then
That he will heed such mandate?   And can I
Resign him if he claims my pledged word?
His hand, not mine, must loose the sacred bond

Which his true love hath wrought—alone deprive
My trembling heart of its last earthly joy,
To be but loved by him.
 Rin.   But I must haste
To bear to him this mandate. Fear not, child,
That I shall influence, I persuade, who mourn
This fatal destiny—whose hopes of bliss
For my last years were all built up with thine,
And see them fallen together ! Fare thee well !

Scene IV.—*Another apartment in the same palace.*

*Alf. (alone; sitting before a table, a letter, with the
 papal seal attached, in his hand).* Oh that this
 brief were but a letter sent
To tell me of her love—to mind me of
The glance that made these dreary scenes so bright,
The vows whose echoes on mine ear return,
Like music heard in dreams ! Oh that it came
To tell me that she loves me still ! Yet that
Would need no written proof; for loving hearts
Speak an unwritten tongue. (*Pauses and looks at the brief
 in deep thought*). I seem to read
The mystery now. Borghese's hand hath moved
My sire's ; my sire's the Pope's. Can this be so ?
Yet can it hardly be. For were it so,
They know too well that I would fling it back
As though it came from some plague-stricken spot.
And what is Rome but that ? Yet let me pause.
How can I bear to bring before her eye
This page, the death-warrant of her true life,

The death-stroke of our love ?   Oh, I should seem
Like heathen monster dragging forth to death
The Christian martyr whose last prayer was raised
For her fell murderer.   Such piteous sight
Might even in savage breast inspire the breath
Of love, or fan the flame of late remorse.
—Laodamia, would I ne'er had loved,
Or loving, had to peasant's life been born,
Whose healthy toil builds up the day in bliss
And crowns the night with rest ; whose love's bright path
Is never crossed by proud ambitions tread ;
Whose heart the fear of poisoned shaft or cup
Can never enter !   But my soul is lost.
I dare not gaze upon the past ; the future
Rises before me, bathes my soul in light,
The glorious baptism of a higher life.   [*Pauses.*
Prince of the Church, I plant my foot upon
The first proud step of my ambition's throne.
Armed with the power which that firm vantage-ground
Will give, and aided by the Sovereign Pontiff,
Siena will fall beneath my sway ; Borghese
Own me his lord—yea, crave his life of me,
Whose death his treacherous hand hath twice essayed.
Then, as a sister, though no more a spouse,
Laodamia shall my glory share,
And the bright vision of my early love
Rise up before me as the form inspired
Of Beatrice filled the heavenly dream
Of Alighieri.—But even now she comes !
Beat low my heart, nor let my stifled breath
Betray the fear, the love that strive to gain
The mastery of my soul !

Enter Laodamia.

Cousin and sister !

Laod. Alfonso, hast thou seen my sire—received
The brief which from the sacred Chancery
He bears thee ?

Alf.   Would that it had never come !
Or else that I could read it as the trick
Of some poor trifler, skilled to counterfeit
The style of Rome.

Laod.   Oh that it were but that !
Then might we smile at it, amused to think
Of that new part thou hast been called to fill
In life's wild drama.   But our time is short ;
We may not waste in converse light these moments
Fraught with strange message both to thee and me.
To me and thee ! for still our lives are one.
Thy griefs, thy joys, are mine ; thy glory still
My morning-star, mine evening-star thy love !

Alf. And hast thou schooled thine heart, Laodamia,
So soon to this dread lesson ?   Mine would seem
Of sterner mould, and harder far to bend.

Laod. The broken spirit hath no need to bend,
The dead to die again ; yet in the faith
That this high destiny will raise thy soul
To higher state, I rise from this deep grave
Of sorrow.   Why should I weigh down thy life
With my poor love ?

Alf.   I pray thee to forbear—
If thou wouldst have me barter thus for glory
The treasure of thy love, Oh, hide from me
The fearful cost !   Speak never of that gift,
Or let me claim it still !

Laod.　　　　　　　　It still is thine,
And I must speak of it that it may yet
Inspire thy life—no more an earthly flame,
But kindled, like the vestal fire of old,
By purest faith, to be extinguished never.
Hear me, then, as with prophet-voice I utter
The last, last charge of this o'erburdened heart,
And let it fire thy soul !

Alf.　　　　　　　　　Oh, tyranny
Of love, still conquering even when yielding up
Its very life, how can I hear thee not ?
How bear to hear thee ?　But thou still must reign.
Now speak.

Laod. Alfonso, God hath called thy soul
To do great work for Him, for Italy,
For our loved country, bleeding with the wounds
Of centuries of wrong.　Rome, Florence, Siena,
What are they all but nests of high-born pirates
Who for mere power would build their houses on
Their country's ruin—write their names in blood,
Then found a dynasty ?　Oh, is not this
The history of our race—the secret spring
Of that dark feud which soon may close its page
With tale of fratricide ?　Was it not this
That armed the Pazzi 'gainst the Medici,
When the great Julian fell beneath the stroke
Of treason, in the very sanctuary ?
'Twas then Lorenzo, o'er his brother's grave,
Spake thus to the full heart of Italy :
"They whom the law for public wrong pursues
Or private guilt, take refuge in the Church
Secure from danger.　What to them gives life,
To us brings death.　Where parricides are safe

The Medici find only murderers." *   [*Pauses.*
And they would shelter thee where Julian fell,
From thy twice-threatened death! and deem my love,
My prayers, my tears, a frailer sanctuary
Than Rome—poor refuge for true hearts like thine.
Is there no dagger there? no hand to wield it?
No church, convenient as the Reparata?
Was not the Pazzi's vengeance armed from thence?
Did not the Pope, Riario, Salviati,†
Wing the dread message and direct the blow?
Yet be it so; weapons of death no more
May be thy safe-guards.   Faith, love, words of peace,
Must be thy daggers now!   (*Pauses in deep emotion, and
    proceeds.*)   Yet hear me further.
Thou wilt be the youngest of the Sacred College,
Yet for that cause the strongest.   Life with them
Is ebbing fast away; with thee its tide
Comes in with the unreined energy of youth.
Theirs is the frothy surf—poor legacy
Of tempests, scattering into clouds of foam
The troubled billows of their lives of guilt,
O'er which thy life, like wave seen far behind,
Shall climb like crest of glory.   Yet beware—

---

* " Sogliono rifuggire nelle chièse tutti quelle, che per pubblica
o privata cagione sono perseguitati.   Adunque da chi gli altri sono
difesi, noi siamo morti; dove i parricidi e gli assassini sono sicuri,
i Medici trovarono gli ucciditori loro" (Machiavelli, " Storia
Fiorent.," l. viii.)

† "Volleno (i Pazzi) avanti alla partita parlasse al Pontefice
(Sisto IV.) il quale fece tutte quelle offerte potette maggiori in
beneficio dell' impresa" ("La congiùra de' Pazzi) (Machiavelli,
"Hist.," li. viii.).   For his complicity in the conspiracy, Riario was
imprisoned, and the Archbishop Salviati, as well as his two brothers,
executed.

C

Their lives were once as thine; thine yet may be
Dispersed in foam, in quicksands lost like theirs.
—Yet one word more.   Alfonso, I have heard thee
Say ofttimes, " May the younger live and flourish !"
What means that doubtful word?   Is it that the young
May live the life of those who went before,
And flourish as they flourished?   Heaven avert
So dire a curse from thee, from Italy,
From all who share our love !   Oh, rather claim
A nobler life—heal wisely; bind in one
The mangled frame of our dear country, torn
As Orpheus was of old, rent limb from limb,
And scattered o'er the wilderness of life !
Oh, gather from their long captivity
The outcasts of our race—our tribes dispersed
In heart, in life, in all but name and place,
Till to the question, " Will ye yet be free,
Be one in glory as in birth and race ?"
The answer shall go forth from thousand tongues
And tens of thousands, "Yes, we will be one
In nation as in tongue—one 'neath the rule
Of that great monarch, whosoe'er he be,
Whom God shall raise among our sons to crown
Our union, and our freedom to restore."
We may not live to hear that rapturous cry,
Yet may we haste its utterance.   Oh, be this
Thy work, be this thy ministry !
    Alf.   I feared
Thy words, Laodamia, lest their burden
Should bear me down with memories of a love
Which fears to live, yet fears still more to die.
But thou hast touched a chord in which our hearts
Beat in strange unison.   Oh, that my soul

Could learn from thine to sacrifice its love
On the high altar of our country's wrongs !
Yet words like these do mind me of my loss,
And rather bind on me an earthly yoke,
Than raise my soul to heaven. An angel's voice
Bids me to rise, yet at that angel's feet
I sink, unnerved and powerless. Even now
My earlier love returns. How dare I climb
To this proud height unless my lifelong guide
Companions me ?
    Laod.   Yet must thou rise to fill
A place of glory in our country's annals,
A glory Siena's lordship could not yield,
Nor my poor love bestow. I may not follow,
Yet from my lowly path in this dim world
My soul shall rise to thee, mine eyes shall gaze,
Yea, till they fail with looking up to thee—
To heaven and thee ; for still my heaven art thou !
And thou wilt think of me with higher love,
Such love as angels bear to us who tread
This lower world ; yea, think of me as one
Who gave thee this high counsel—all, all else
Forget for ever ; deem it ne'er has been,
Thy wrongs, thy grief—
    Alf.   —But never yet my love.!

END OF ACT I.

ACT II.

SCENE I.—*Rome. The apartments of* RINALDO *in the Vatican. An oratory with altar and crucifix,* LAODAMIA *kneeling before it.*

Laod. I have no more to give—no second life,
No higher love; my lifelong passionday
Hath brought no Easter-tide.   From morn to morn
I bear my cross, as though the death-strewn path
To Calvary for me might never end.
Oh that this heart in its dread loneliness
Could feel that all "is finished "—fear and doubt,
And life and love—the tale of grief all told !
Yet for a father's sake, a sister's love——
  Viol. (entering unobserved).   Laodamia !
  Laod.   Oh, why hast thou broken
My dream of misery?   Why wake me up
To prove it is not all a dream ?   For thee
I made that sacrifice : for him—for thee.
Was the frail censer of this heart unhallowed,
That Heaven rejects it still?
  Viol.   My sister, say,
What meanest thou ?
  Laod.   Alfonso's hate still burns.
The purple yet may bear the stain of blood ;
My offering yet be fruitless.

Viol.   Yet for me
Was that peace-offering made.   Oh that thy love
Had never made it—that it still could live
To mould Alfonso's life !   Alas ! the feud
Made now inveterate through the friendship formed
With the crafty Cardinal de' Medici,
Hath severed him from thee as from Borghese—
From all his house, and mine, alas ! still dimmed
By the dread memories of that day of guilt
When the great Julian fell   Thou know'st the hate
Which fires my uncle 'gainst the Medici ;
How hardly he escaped the avenging blow
When the fierce Pazzi sowed that seed of blood,
Whose harvest we have reaped in our sad lives.
Yet now Alfonso, mindless of the laws
Of Holy Church, and of the oath he took
As Cardinal, molests the electors' ears
With base solicitations, and their souls
Corrupts with promises of place and power,
If they but raise the foe of all his race
To fill the papal throne.
     Rin. (entering in an excited state). There is a fearful
          tumult in the piazza.
Loud curses load the memory of Julius.
His buried life is writ in deeds of blood ;
His memory lives in curses, loudly uttered
By those his fierce ambition hath bereaved
Of husbands, sons, and brothers—fruitless seed !
Yea, rather, rich with harvest of despair.
Our Italy, which through a thousand wounds
Poured out her life blood to cement his throne,
Now sinks exhausted, prostrate at the feet
Of tyrants whose sole power is in her weakness,

Whose only gain her loss.* But hark! the crowd
Surges beneath us; let us gaze on it
From yonder balcony.

> [*A curtain is withdrawn, disclosing an open balcony
> overlooking the great courtyard of the Vatican.*
> RINALDO, *with* LAODAMIA *and* VIOLANTE,
> *fall back upon it.*

Rin. See this wild scene! look yonder! Who is that
Appearing from the portals of the conclave
And hasting to the front? It is Alfonso!
With wild excitement he hath thrust aside
The officers appointed to proclaim
The future Pontiff. Hear you not his voice?

Alf. (*from the opposite balcony*). The Medici is Pope!
    Lorenzo's son,
Great-grandson of the noble Cosimo!
Pope by a vote unanimous! Long live
The young! "*Vivant vigeantque juniores!*" †

Rin. (*coming forward*). These fifty years I have been
    Prothonotary
Of the Holy See, yet never saw I such
A scene as this—the sacred suffrage cast
Like thing profane upon the populace,
And trampled under foot. Oh, shame and grief!
Alfonso, Cardinal, sworn to secrecy,
Claiming the guidance of the Holy Ghost.
For this dread work, yet standing forth as prince

---

* Guicciardini observes that Julius's memory "was honoured most
by those who held it to be more the duty of the Popes to increase
the authority of the Apostolic See by warfare and the blood of Chris-
tians, than to promote it by the example of a good life" (l. xi.).

† Leo X. was thirty-seven years old, Petrucci was twenty-six, in
the year 1513. For the description of this scene, see Palatius in his
life of Leo X.

Of Holy Church proclaiming to the world
The lust of power and place, the worship of
A name which soon may shroud in infamy
The dying glories of his house and race !

Alf. (entering and seeing only LAODAMIA). Laodamia !
The game is won.   The Medici hath triumphed ;
Siena may yet be mine !

Rin.   Are these the words
Of priest, of bishop,* prince of Holy Church ?
—Oh, wreck of that high soul which once aspired
To deeds that would have made thy name immortal,
Now sunk in guilt and shame, by lust of power
Degraded, and with base corruption stained !

Alf. Rinaldo, this from thee?   Were it not that thou
Might'st once have been my sire, and still dost bear
That name for this dear object of my love,
This arm had laid thee at the feet of him
Thy words have wronged, of him who scorns thy trade.
Go preach thy drivelling law pontifical
To other ears than mine.

Laod.   Alfonso, stay
Thy guilty wrath, and though I scorn to plead
The love thou barest me once, I yet would claim
Thy reverence for the hoary locks that crown
A father's brow, a worthier diadem
Than that which thy insatiate pride would snatch
Even at Pandolfo's grave.

Alf.   Laodamia,
I have been wild and rash, and though thy speech
Pierces my heart—and oh, that heart still loves,
And still can feel the shaft of love's reproach—
Forgive me !

* Alfonso Petrucci had been made Bishop of Saona.

Laod.   Would that on Borghese's heart
That pitying glance could fall as now on mine !
That the bright day when all our race was one
Might dawn on us again ! that we might never
Say with La Pia, " Siena gave us life,
But the Maremma of revenge and hate
Unmade what God had wrought." *   Thou yet mayst
        haste
That day's glad advent hour, whose morn would spread
A firmament of peace o'er all our lives.
Forgive Borghese's wrongs, and make thyself
Invincible through love, in mercy's realm
A conqueror and a prince.
    Alf.   I was not born ·
For saintly crown.   The glory that encircles
The martyr's brow accords not with the hat
Of Cardinal, called to rule and not to suffer.
Yet if my soul could change, and love could reign
In every thought, to thine importunate prayers,
Not to my will, the heavenly work were due.   [*Pauses.*
—Oh, guardian angel of this life of guilt,
Could I but rise with thee—with thee look down
Upon this lower world !   Alas, my soul
Cleaveth unto the dust,† and yet would cling
Even as the dust unto the feet of her
Whose love shall be my life's last minister.
Rinaldo, give me but thy hand, thy blessing ;

----

* " Ricorditi di me che son la Pia,
        Siena mi fè, disfece mi Maremma. '
                        DANTE, *Purg.*, v. 133.

† " *Adhæsit pavimento anima mea.*"
    " Sentià dir lor con sì alti sospieri
        Che la parola appena s' intendea."
                        DANTE, *Purg.*, c. xix. v. 73.

Violante, let me learn in loving thee
To love the brother who hath wronged me most,
Who twice essayed my life.

Enter a Messenger.

                        But who is this
Disturber of our privacy? What message
Bearest thou from the Conclave?
  Mess.   Eminence,
The Holy Father, Pontiff now elect,
Desires thy presence and thine homage claims
To-morrow in the hall of the Consistory.
  Alf. I will obey the call.
  Laod.   Oh, arm thyself
With high restraint; let no unwonted joy,
Like that which fired thee first, betray thee now.
Be worthy of thy name, and of thy place
In this great household. Let the Medici
See that the race they hate is worthy yet
To reign in Rome, as it hath reigned in Siena.

    .

Scene II.—*The Pope's private apartments in the Vatican.*
    Leo X.; Raffaello Petrucci. *Raffaello is read-
ing to the Pope the Annals of Florence.*

  Leo X. What wondrous words! as though the Seraph's
    hand
Had touched his lips with fire from off the altar,
Even as the Prophet's. Read me them again.
  Raff. (*reads*). "Think, mighty citizens, to what dread
    straits
An evil fortune hath led on our house,

When even 'midst friends and kindred, yea, and in
The Church itself, our life was not secure." *

Leo X. Even of ourselves how true! This great Basilica,
The heart and centre of our Christendom,
May be to me as the Church of the Reparata
Was to my father—an Aceldama!
I know that I am walking o'er the graves
Of murdered Pontiffs, princes of the Church,
Actors or victims in the fatal deeds
Which fill these halls with memories of the slain
By sword, by poison, or by base intrigue,†
Whose souls cry out from 'neath our altar-stones,
" How long, O God, how long?" Nor faith, nor love,
Nor conscious innocence can here find place,
Yet is our trust in God.

Raff. That vantage-ground
Is thine alone, for none trusts in Him here.

Leo X. How can they, when the spirit of the Pazzi
Lives in their hearts, and fires their frenzied eye!
Look at the time-worn Cardinal Riario,
Friend and accomplice of that dread design;
Did not the Pope his uncle, and his friend,
The tyrant Julius, wage incessant war
Against our house—invoke the emperor's arms
To crush the rising liberties of Florence?
Read me Lorenzo's words.

---

* " Considerate, magnifici Cittadini, dove la cattiva fortuna aveva
condotta la casa nostra, che fra gli amici, fra i parenti, nella chiesa
non era sicura" (Machiavelli, *ut suprà*).

† Leo himself is believed to have been poisoned (Eggs, *Pontificium
Doctum*, pag. 706). Julius II. died of grief and vexation at his
political reverses. Pius III. is supposed to have been poisoned at
the instance of Pandolfo Petrucci. Alexander VI. was poisoned in
his own attempt to poison the richer Cardinals.

Raff. (*reads*)   "Why should they form
Alliance with the Pope; league with the King
Of Naples 'gainst the sacred liberties
Of this republic ?   Wherefore break the long
Calm peace of Italy ?" *

Leo X.   One only link
Fails in this chain of treason !   They have got
No Julius on this throne.   No Sixtus builds
His treacherous plans against our house.   Yet still
The Kings of France and Naples, yea, the cities
Free (as they term them) of our Italy,
For ever prone to shed Italian blood,
Are leagued against us.   Even thy native Siena,
Scene of our exile, whence we watched the sun
Rise upon Florence, make her loveliness
More lovely, while it gilded all her domes,
As though the heaven itself had blushed to see
Its glories still surpassed—even Siena now,
Beneath Pandolfo's rule, Borghese's hate,
Affianced as he is to a Riario,
Warns us of hidden danger.

Raff.   Thou hast touched
A chord of grief to which my heart responds
In concord of an anguish deeper still.
Already bent in weariness of death,
Pandolfo lies, and prays that his spent life
May pass away to man's eternal rest,
Ere he beholds his son a fratricide—
Ere the third stroke of fierce Borghese's knife
Pierces the breast of him he loves the most,

* ."Perchè far lega con il Papa, e con il Rè contro alla libertà
di questa Repubblica? perchè rompere la lunga pace d' Italia?"
(Machiavelli, *ut suprà*).

Yet dreads to see.   Alfonso soon will claim
The licence of your Holiness to leave
Your Court for a brief season, to attend
The death-bed of his sire.   Oh, grant it not !
Reasons of state, and perils scarce foreseen
By keenest eye, forbid such journey now.
If once let loose, like tameless beasts of prey,
The brothers soon would join in fearful onslaught,
And Siena rise in wild revolt to claim
Her ancient freedom.

    Leo X.   I will heed thy words
Of wisdom, prudent aye, and opportune,
And stand forearmed against the treacherous plea
Of Don Alfonso.   But our time is short.
The homage hour, with bitter memories fraught
And shrouded in dark prophecies of guilt,
Approaches.   Would that it brought open war,
Instead of utterance of unfelt devotion ;
Then should I welcome it.

    Mess.   Most Holy Father,
The Sacred College waits with reverence meet
For the high presence of your Holiness.

    Leo X. We are prepared ; lead on.   [*Exeunt.*

SCENE III.—*Apartments of* RIARIO *in the Vatican.*
    CARDINAL RIARIO, VIOLANTE, *afterwards* BORGHESE.

    Viol. My uncle, thou art pale.   This homage-day
Hath been too long for thee.   Thy breath seems short ;
Now rest thee, nor attempt too soon to tell
The tale of this day's work.

    Ria.   Loved Violante,

The music of thy voice brings back my soul
Into sweet concord with that peaceful life,
Which, through my downward years of guilt and grief,
Hath run like placid stream through dark ravine,
Luring the sunbeam which the towering crags
Lose in their deep recesses, and reflecting
The rays that should have lighted first on them.
But is Borghese here?   I fain would tell
My weary tale but once.
  Viol.   Even now he comes.

     Enter Borghese.

 Ria. The homage of this day bodes ill to all
Who bear our name.   Attended by Raffaello
The Pontiff entered the Consistory ;
With proud sardonic smile he gazed around
And muttered words of welcome.   When I knelt
Before him, with brief speech assuring him
Of tried fidelity, with bitter smile
He said, "We do accept this tribute new
Of the good faith of the Riarii
To us and all our house."   I know not what
I spake, but what I thought is fresh as when
It flashed as lightning through my fevered brain.
It was—I dared not utter it—the wish   .
That when the Pazzi struck the uncle down,
The sire had fallen as well,—that all the race
Had perished on that day.   '
  Viol.   The Lord absolve thee
From such dark thought of guilt.   But oh, proceed.
What said the Pontiff more?
  Ria.   The homages

Which followed gave worse omen.   Soderini
Implored the Pope to aid his exiled brother
And order his return to Florence.   Vain
His suit ; the Pontiff coldly turned away !
Then proudly rose the Cardinal, his kinsman,
And muttered words of ill-concealed revenge.

    Viol. It bodes us ill, my uncle ; but speak on.

    Ria. After some speechless greetings, whispered low
By men who seemed to tremble lest their voice
Should echo the dread words their ears had heard
And their faint hearts affirmed, yet dared not speak,
Alfonso knelt before the Pope, and sought
His licence to retire awhile to Siena
And tend his dying sire.

    Viol.   And did the Pope
Grant his untimely prayer ?

    Ria.   With firmer tone
Than yet had marked his speech, the Pope replied,
" It may not be.   Reasons of state require
Thy presence now with us, and Siena needs
Rest from the weary conflict of her sons,
Thy sire a peaceful death."   'Twas then Alfonso
Cast on the Pope so fierce a glance, it seemed
As though the steel he bears beneath his cloak
Had flashed from out his eyes.   What words he spake
I heard not.   But I saw the Pope turn round
To Don Raffaello and thus speak aside ;
" I do mislike his words ; they seem to me
To savour of the treason of the Pazzi.
Didst ever hear such tones of proud disdain
Uttered to Sovereign Pontiff ? "

    Borg.   Would that he
Would turn upon the hated Medici

The wrath that once was fiercely turned on us !
Dishonoured love begets inveterate hate ;
Inveterate hate, revenge.   Then other hands
Would do my work—the third stroke better aimed
Prove fatal.

    Viol.   Oh, forbear !   Forgive, kind Heaven,
That murderous thought !   Alas ! our very prayers
Are turned to imprecations, and our blessings
Yield us but curses ; yea, our bitter lives
Do poison all we love !   Is there no branch
Of healing we might cast into the waters
Of this dread strife, to sweeten and to bless ?

    Ria. There is the blessed cross ! but we have lost
That holy birthright, and its blessing now
Hath passed from us for ever !

SCENE IV.—*An apartment in the Vatican.*   ALFONSO ;
SODERINI ; SAULIO.

    Alf. 'Twas but the difference of age and youth,
Young and old Italy, that severed us ;
But now the consciousness of common wrong,
The thirst for common vengeance, makes us one.

    Sau. Said I not that thy prayer would turn again
To thine own bosom—to the Pope fulfilled
In blessing ; to thyself, to us, a curse !
The young still flourishes, but not in thee—
Still lives, but not for thee, and thou art cast
On us the aged, as a wave-worn wreck
Upon a desert coast.   In Leo's soul
Age finds no reverence, youth no sympathy.
We have a merchant Pope ; mean hucksterer

For place and power, even as his sire and grandsire,
Who dazzled Florence with their sordid gifts,
Till it was blinded to receive their yoke.
Would that their golden fetters were not forged
For us as for the Florentines.

Alf.   'Tis ours
To break them off us with a stronger hand
Than that which laid the haughty Julian low.
This dagger is not borne in vain !   [*Produces a dagger.*

Sau. and Sod. (together).   Great God !

Sod. Dost wear the weapon of a murderer ?

Sau. The argument of the wild Trasteverini,
The message of the Pazzi ? *

Alf.   Craven hearts !
And did not Brutus gain the patriot's crown
By tempered steel like this—by mighty heart
Tempered as was his steel ? yea, sharpened, too,
With wrongs and insults lighter far than those
Which give their edge to this !

Sod.   Insensate boy !
Thine untrained youth, which with importunate zeal
Did raise the Medici to this great throne
From which his pride hath spurned thee, now would
          crown
His recreant soul with martyrdom, and clothe
Thine own with infamy ; yea, give a saint
To that detested house, and add to thine
A murderer.

Alf.   I would the leach who treats
The Pontiff for some ailment, could but mix

---

* Two of that great family, even in earlier days, had been involved
in murders—Rinier Pazzi and Camicion de' Pazzi, both placed by
Dante in his " Inferno " (cant. xii. 137, and xxxii. 68).

His soothing draught with skill—some potent drug
Distil in greater strength, some pharmacy
In over-dose dispense, perchance of purpose,
Or, haply, by mistake.
    Sau.   Forbear, forbear !
We dare not hear such speech.   Unsay thy words,
Or teach us to forget them.
    Alf.   Wipe them out
From your weak memories ; suffer not a word,
A whisper from your lips, a troubled look,
The mystery of my vengeance to reveal.
Remember Julian's fate, the Pazzi's dagger,
The countless paths which in these silent walls
Have led to fearful death !   [*Exit.*
    Sau.   How fierce his look !
A frenzy of despair distorts his soul.
Dare we be silent ?
    Sod.   Yet how dare we speak !
To hide within our breasts the fearful secret,
Or to reveal it, both were certain death !
Seek we the prudent counsel of Riario,
Skilled in the windings of that maze of guilt
In which our lives are cast—each treacherous turn,
Each hidden pitfall.   But the time is short ;
Haste we to meet him ere the ripening plot
Bears fruits of poison both for thee and me.
    Sau. Thy speech is wise : we dare not waste an hour.
We have heard more than we can dare conceal,
Yet how reveal it?   [*Exeunt.*

END OF ACT II.

D

ACT III.

Scene I.—*Siena. An apartment in the palace of the Petrucci.* Pandolfo, *lying on a couch, attended by* Borghese *and* Violante; *the* Archbishop of Siena *standing by him.*

Pan. (with eyes closed, starting convulsively). It is Alfonso's step ! take—take him from me.
Violante, art thou near me ?   Stand between them ;
Beneath the mantle of the Cardinal
He hides the dagger.*
Viol.   Father, 'tis not he :
Borghese only stands beside thee now.
Pan. (still with closed eyes, and covering his face with his hand).   A name of death !   He bore it once who bore
A father's name for me ;† he bears it now

---

* " Alphonsus . . . pugionem clam in cardinalium
    Conventu sæpius tulisse fertur."
                    Palatius in " Vita Leonis X."

† " Diventato maggiore Pandolfo potette poco poi fare ammazzare il suocero che troppo arditamente attraversava i suoi disegni " (Guicciardini, lix.).

Who bears the blade which through Alfonso's heart
Must pierce my own!   Oh, 'tis a name of death!
                                        [*Pauses.*
Say you Borghese only stands beside me?
It is not he.   No, no, my Violante;
I see the blood-stain.   Murder cannot sleep,
Nor murdered rest; in mortal sin he died.
He fell unshriven!   Look, look; he rises there!
He stands before me!   Now his sightless orbs
Are turned upon me!   Niccolò Borghese,
Thou art avenged!   (*Wakes up and continues, after a
     pause*) Oh, good Lord Archbishop,
Thou read'st as in the Prophet's mystic roll
The secret will of Heaven.   Say, can my sons
Live to bear on the standard of our race
When this poor hand is cold and stiff in death?
     Archb. The dying hand should only grasp the cross;
The standard which thy glorious ancestors
Bare when they led the soldiers of the faith
Up to the earthly Sion.   They have gone
Before thee to the City of the King,
Vision of peace——
     Pan.   But of despair for me!
     Archb. Oh, Lord Pandolfo, lift thine eyes to Heaven,
From whence cometh thy help.   Look not behind,
And stay not in the plain of these dread thoughts,
Lest thou reach not the only city of refuge
For sin-sick souls.   Oh, let me give to thee
The sweet Viaticum.
     Pan.   I dare not lift
My heart to Heaven.   My soul in its last throes
Cleaveth unto the dust, and—to—Alfonso!
Poor boy, I loved him once!

Borg. (*aside to* VIOLANTE). And loves him still !
Violante, is that writing signed ?

    Viol.   We sought
To make him sign it, but in vain !   His hand
Shook like a leaf in autumn.

    Borg.   Yet on that
Hangs all our future.   Haste, and bring it hither.

    Viol. How can I leave him ?

    Borg.   Then myself I go,
Else will he die intestate.   Even if sight
Have failed, his mind is clear ; we yet might guide
His trembling hand.

    Pan. (*awaking to consciousness, but with his eyes still
         closed*). Oh, is it my Alfonso ?
Dear heart ! how like the angel form that bare him,-
Who, when her love forgave me my great guilt,
Prayed that my heart might never share her grief,
Or doubt her faith !   Had she been with us still,
To kindle with her love our cold spent lives,
Borghese would have never sought thy life,
My son, nor thou his birthright !

    Archb.   Oh, be calm.
Alfonso is not here, and she thou lovedst
Is now a saint in heaven, and bids thee rise,
That where thy treasure is, thy heart may be—
With her !

    Pan.   With her ?   Oh, resurrection-life !
She lifts me from the grave, I rise, I live,
Alfonso, is this death ?

    Alf. (*enters suddenly*). My father, speak !
Say—say I am forgiven.

    Pan.   Can love say less ?
Oh, God ! the death-sleep comes !   [*Dies.*

Borg. (*re-entering with a parchment, but not seeing*
ALFONSO).   Doth he yet live?

Archb. Read you not on his face the lines of death?
Oh, pray we for his rest.

Borg.   Say you he's dead?
And this is yet unsigned!

Alf.   My signature,
Perchance, may give it force, or I might write
My name as witness that it ne'er was signed.

Borg. Base felon, from thy papal chain escaped,
How darest thou break the oath that binds thee to
The Pope thyself hast made!

Archb.   Dare you, rash youths,
Even in this presence-chamber of grim death
To bandy words of warfare, when the lips
Of him whose blessing fell on both alike
Are scarcely cold?

Viol.   Oh, holy archbishop,
Forgive their reckless guilt, and raise thy prayers
For them—for him whose soul in purging flames
Is now enwrapped.   They know not what they say;
They dare not what they will!

Archb.   Poor child, thine heart
Is all too great for theirs.   Of one, at least,
Thou art the guardian angel.   But a troop
Of sad domestics comes—poor, simple souls!—
To do the last sad rites of watchful care
For him they loved not in his day of life,
Yet mourn in the night of death.   Let us retire.

Scene II.—*The Senate House in Siena. The* Secretary
   of the Republic, Borghese, Alfonso, Archbishop,
   Senators, *and* Citizens.

Sec. The closing scene of Don Pandolfo's life
Comes on us sadly, yet not suddenly.
His day of doom was late ; the shock was ripe,
Yet unprepared the ground for other seedtime.
'Tis for yourselves, most noble citizens
Met in full senate, either to invite
Another lord to rule ye, or resolve
To cultivate the field of Siena's glory
With the skilled hands which sowed in earlier day
Seed of great deeds whose harvest others reaped,
Making your sons mere labourers in the field
Bought with their father's blood.
   Borg.   Oh, faithful sons
Of Siena, can ye hear such words unmoved
With indignation, uttered o'er the grave
Of him who was your friend, your counsellor ?
   The Crowd. Our tyrant and our curse !
   Borg.   Say you your curse ?
Him who with hollow hearts ye blessed in life
Ye curse amid the awful calm of death—
Dumb dogs, who dared not bark while yet he lived,
And now, unmuzzled, bite !
   The Crowd.   The living dog
Is better than dead lion.
   Borg.   Have a care ;
The lion's heart is here, and growling curs
May wake it soon to life.

Alf.   Loved citizens,
If words like these fire not your souls with wrath
Too deep for utterance, hear me not this day ;
But if they teach you what my life hath been
In the hard bondage of this fratricide,
Who twice hath sought my life, then list to me
While o'er my father's grave I plead my cause
And claim my rights.
    Borg.   What rights can younger son
Claim o'er his elder ?
    The Crowd.   Hear the Don Alfonso ;
He hath been ever proved the people's friend.
    Alf. My utterance must be short.   In yonder palace
Death reigns supreme.   Beneath the dim horizon
Which hedges in our life, my sire's hath fallen ;
But as though highest Heaven had interposed
To make his glorious countrymen his heirs,
His will is yet unsigned.   Whate'er that will
Appointed is as void as though it ne'er
Were writ.
    Borg.   False traitor to thy name and race,
Thou liest !   This sacred testament, declared
In the presence of the Lord Archbishop's grace,
Proclaims me as his heir.
    Sec.   Produce the will.
We have legal experts here whose skill might test it.
    Borgh. Perish your experts !   My great father's will,
Writ by the sword, doth need the sword alone
As its interpreter.
    Alf.   That key to read
Unwritten law is ours, not less than yours ;
And we may claim it too.
    Sec.   Most noble sirs,

Our Senate meets for higher work than this.
'Tis for this great assembly to determine
If they will have another lord to rule
In Siena, or will here resume and now
The ill-deputed charge.   Are any here
For Don Borghese ?   Any to propose
The Lord Alfonso, Prince and Cardinal
Of Holy Church ?
    A voice.   I claim your suffrages
For the true heir, Borghese.
    Another.   And I ask
Your votes for Don Alfonso—tried and true,
The people's friend.
    Archb.   And I, as legate born
Of the Apostolic See, propound the will
Of the chief Pontiff, that the heritage
Of Lord Pandolfo, forfeit through the guilt
And conflict of his sons, shall now devolve
On Don Raffaello, brother of Pandolfo,
Their natural uncle.   His supreme decree
I here produce, and in his name declare
The Lord Raffaello lord and prince in Siena !
    Sec.   And I, this Senate's representative
And secretary, set aside thy claim,
Annul thy suit, pronounce it openly
Void and of none effect ; and I do here
Suspend this sitting till the funeral rites
Of Don Pandolfo have been solemnized,
And we can meet, unbribed and unconstrained,
To claim our rights, as only lawful heirs
Of our intestate lord.
             [The assembly breaks up in confusion.

SCENE III.—*A chamber lighted with numerous tapers.*
The coffin of DON PANDOLFO *in the centre, surrounded*
by attendants watching. ALFONSO ; BORGHESE.

Alf. Faithful retainers of our father's house,
For a brief season we would be alone
In this dark scene of death.
   Borg.   Let us, my friends,
Relieve your pious watch, that ye may rest
While we, with saddened hearts, do meditate
O'er this dear corpse.
   Attendants.   We will retire, my lord.
                     [*Exeunt* Attendants.
   Alf. Brother—unwonted word, yet not unblessed,
When uttered o'er his corpse to whom we owe
Our life, our name, our race !—too long our hearts
By bitter rivalry and causeless hate
Have been asunder rent.   Now, as we stand
At the dread portal of a father's grave,
Oh, let the past be past, our hatred sheathed
In love or mild forgetfulness of wrong.
For us, our sire lives still.   Raffaello's claim
Insults his name and birthright.   From the grave
That voice which oft hath called us to the field
Now summons us to vengeance ; bids us list
'Neath the same banner—soldiers, friends, and brothers.
   Borg. I joy to hear thee claim a brother's name,
Even though the sympathy of a common hate
Were all that joined our hearts.   And yet, Alfonso,
Time was when, in the innocence of youth
And in the simple bond of childlike faith,
Unenvying and unenvied, we were one.

In every feat of arms, or martial game,
We were competitors ; yet love was still
The prize for which we fought, the crown we won.
Oh, 'twas an evil day in which I writ
Upon thy breast the record of my guilt,
And of thy wrong—alas ! yet unforgiven.

   Alf. Oh, deem it now atoned, or rather read it
As covenant of peace, witness of love,
Writ with a brother's blood.

   Borg.   I will, I will ;
For with one word thy love hath gently stanched
The deeper wound of guilty consciousness
Of such fell deed.   Give me thine hand as pledge
Of faith renewed.

   Alf.   I will ; yet were it ill
To yield these moments, sacred to stern thought,
Even to the accents of returning love !
Raffaello hath usurped our heritage,
And the base Medici, who owes his throne
To me, casts off the allegiance of my faith,
Spurns from his feet the friend who raised him up
Even from the dust ; but his vile life shall pay
The forfeit of his treachery !

   Borg.   I hate,
Like thee, the Pope and all his merchant crew,
And fain would see Riario on the throne
His uncle filled, who loved our sire so well
And was his trusted friend.   Yet were it ill
To waste our wrath on him.   I care but little
Who reigns in Rome ; my war-cry is but this—
The foul usurper ne'er shall reign in Siena.

   Alf. Yet *must* he reign, while reigns in Rome the Medici
That reign must first be closed.

   Borg.   What meanest thou ?

Alf. Wouldst thou dry up the stream?   Quench first
    the source.
Or kill the tree?   Cut off its hidden root.
Dethrone Raffaello?   First dethrone the Pope
Who raised him up to cast thee in the dust.
    Borg. I dare not follow thee in path like this.
Base as he is, he is the successor
Of Peter, God's vicegerent.   I would wage
Incessant war against his temporal reign;
Invoke the powers of heaven and earth to join
To drive him from our Italy, to force him
To prove his kingdom is not of this world,
His weapons not from hence; yet ne'er could I
Lift up my hand to take his life.   Great God!
My arm would wither up; my heart would fail.
He is the Lord's anointed.
    Alf.   Weak in heart,
And weak in memory too!   Hast never read
How many a fabled successor of Peter
Hath gently slept his poisonous life away
Through potent drug by friendly hand dispensed?
Did not the Borgia, but a few years hence,
Drink the empoisoned cup by skilful hand
Mixed, but by hand less prudent ministered?
Mine be that skill, while thy revenge o'ertakes
The fell usurper in the open field
Thy warlike soul loves best.
    Borg.   My work is clear.
I haste this day to claim the proffered aid
Of the King of Naples; from his Court I pass
To the Most Christian King, whose eager hate
Seeks a just pretext for long-threatened war
With Florence and the Medici.
    Alf.   'Twere well

That I should wait thee here, and watch the game
By Don Raffaelo played.   [*A* Messenger *enters.*
    Messenger.   His Holiness
Charged me to give this brief into your hands,
Lord Cardinal, and command your swift return.
Your absence is unlicensed, and the needs
Of Church and State require your Eminence
To speed your course to Rome.
    Alf. (*reads the brief*).   Go, tell your master
Our Court at Siena needs our presence more,
But—— (*Aside*) I must needs dissemble.   (*To the*
        Messenger) I obey.
Borghese, 'tis for thee to plead our cause
In Siena ; mine to vindicate our rights
Even at the fountain-head of guilt and wrong,
At Rome !   [*Exeunt.*

Scene IV.—*A public place in Siena.   Two* Citizens.

    1*st Cit.* What these wild shouts ? this crowding in the
        streets ?
This rush to gain the Senate house ?
    2*nd Cit.*   I marvel
That thou hast heard not.   Raffaello came
This morn from Rome, to take his place among
The mourners at his brother's funeral—
Came with the papal brief which made him heir
To Siena's lordship ; with the ensigns, too,
Of Cardinal (for the Pope to force his claim
Hath raised him to the purple), and with train
Of followers armed, and (as it seemed) prepared
To fright away or else to quell resistance.

But scarce had he arrived before the gates,
Which the vast crowd assembled to behold
The dreary pageant made impassable,
When such a rush was made on every side
That he was forced to beat a quick retreat,
The furious throng pursuing, and dividing
Between the living tyrant and the dead
Such threats and curses as were never heard
Uttered o'er vilest bandit.

    1st Cit.   What befel
The funeral-car and its long cavalcade
Of mourners hired to mourn?

    2nd Cit.   They sped their way
Into a by-street leading towards the back
Of the cathedral, and the angry crowd
Cared not to follow.

    1st Cit.   But the bell that calls
The senators sounds from the Campanile.

    2nd Cit. Thy fears have given it voice; I hear it not.

    1st Cit. Can it be Don Pandolfo's funeral bell?
Yet that would be of deeper tone.   Again
I hear it.   From the Senate house it sounds!

    2nd Cit. Thou hast a sharper ear than mine.   That note
Must haste our steps, if we would stem the tide
Which pours from every street and lane to meet
In wildest concourse in the market-place.
Moments are days; our freedom soon must be
Weighed in the balance 'gainst a tyrant's claim.
A single vote may turn the trembling scale.
Oh, let us haste our steps; the surging crowd
Will soon close o'er our path.   The bell hath ceased!
                            [Exeunt.

END OF ACT III.

ACT IV.

Scene I.—*Rome. An apartment of* Cardinal Riario *in the Vatican.* Alfonso; Riario.

Ria. Forget that he was born a Medici;
In the ascent to the Pontifical throne,
Name, race, and all the accidents of birth
Are lost, or pale as dim and distant lights,
In that exceeding glory.
    Alf.   Foolish thought!
And deem'st thou that he will so soon forget
That thou art a Riario; that thine uncle,
Even though he sate on Peter's sacred throne,
Joined with the Pazzi in their bold attempt
To stamp out from the earth his name and race?
Will he forget that thou wert leagued with those
Who bore the avenging knife when Julian fell?
    Ria. Why lead my steps, fast verging on the grave,
To that dread charnel-house? Oh, let the past
Be past indeed!
    Alf.   And is the present, then,
Fraught with no dangers? Is our future life
Peaceful and cloudless as the summer's sky?
Seest thou not that he only bides his time
To strike, whilst thou art creeping to the grave,
Or lowly crouching to receive the blow?

Oh, prove thy right to bear a glorious name,*
Which else shall live but in the lying page
Of hated Machiavel.
 Ria.   Young man, thy words
Fall on mine ear like voices from the dead,
Bringing back memories of a grisly past.
Oh, shut them up within thy breast, and spare
This frame, fast sinking in the calm of death
And craving only peace.
 Alf.   And wouldst thou seek
Peace at the price of honour—endless shame
For a few hours of base inglorious rest?
 Ria. Forbear, and force me not, by that firm oath
We took to guard the Pontiff's sacred life
And to reveal its dangers, to disclose
Thy words of hideous guilt.
 Alf.   If thou but breathe
One word, the dagger which must pierce his breast
Shall first be sheathed in thine.
 Ria.   Impetuous youth,
Think'st thou that I, a Roman, fear to meet
A Roman's death? Alas! the assassin's knife
In Rome may meet our breast at every step,
The poisoned cup approach our lips in house
Of friends—accustomed hospitality.
Sheathe, then, thy dagger, or go forth to join
The wild Trasteverini in their strifes,
And dare not to a prince of Holy Church
Disclose a bandit's guilt.

---

 * The origin of the Riario family is rather obscure. Raffaello
Riario was the son of Antonio Sansone by Violante Riario, the near
relation of Pope Sixtus IV. That Pope adopted him as a nephew,
and enjoined on him the assumption of the name and arms of Riario.

Alf.   Thy words are brave;
Yet, if thou prize the few fast-running sands
Of thy life's glass, be voiceless as the grave,
Which else will close on thee before thy time,
To teach eternal silence.   [*Exit.*

SCENE II.—*Apartments of* ALFONSO. ALFONSO; VER-
    CELLI. ANTONIO *at a table, writing.*

Alf. How fares the Holy Father?
Ver.   If the fears
And anxious cares that load a Pontiff's life
Could find relief, I ween he would fare well.
Alf. But hath he cause for fear?
Ver.   Your Eminence
Must better know than I do.   On the day
Of the Consistory, an ague chill
Came o'er him, and a flush of heat, like that
Which Romans know too well, succeeded it.
Alf. Yet simplest remedies might well reduce
Such symptom—some narcotic wisely mixed,
Producing welcome sleep.   What think'st thou, doctor?
Ver. I dare not treat his case, as I might treat
The poor Trasteverine's, whose vile frame
I might experiment upon; yea, prove
The strength of poisonous drugs to test their use.
Alf. Yet have the Medici a charmèd life.
No Roman, like Lorenzo, could have braved
The Pazzi's dagger, or outlived its wound;
And nerves like these, when weakened and unstrung,
Do need strong remedies.   Dost heed my meaning?

Ver. Strong remedy might kill ; mere soothing draught
Bring short relief. A middle course were better ;
And that would best sustain his confidence
In us, and best prolong a life which yet
May yield a fruitful harvest to our skill.

Alf. Yet in a field where patient care and skill
Too oft is unrewarded, and tried service
Meets cold neglect or base ingratitude,
The harvest of thy skill may yet be reaped
By other hands than thine.

Ver.   What means my lord?

Alf. Plain speech were dangerous. And yet the
          thought
That if the Pazzi in an earlier day,
Instead of rushing madly to the slaughter,
Had mixed the—the—the bowl of aconite
Or deadly henbane, they had reigned in Florence,
And Rome had never seen a Medici.

Ver. Yet oft the poisoned cup hath missed its aim,
As in the Borgias' case.

Alf.   'Twas ill conceived ;
They overreached themselves. The poisoned wine
Was sent too soon. Such half-begotten crimes
Die in the birth ; the finished work alone
Is crowned with honour.

Ver.   Yet if it should fail?

Alf. It cannot fail, unless the recreant heart
Fail first, the hand unnerved refuse its work.
Fortune, like willing slave, waits on success
And crowns its finished work. (*In an undertone*) The
          half-wrought deed
Of Florence must be finished here in Rome.
Dost understand my meaning?

                                        E

Ver.   For myself,
If I had planned that work I would have wrought it
With better skill than his who weakly shrank
From the death-deed, and saved Lorenzo's life.
And yet their fate who rushed to that dark fray
Untimely, and were all red-handed seized,
And paid the forfeit of their guilt, might daunt
The bravest of their followers.   Nor the rank
Of Salviati, nor Riario's power,
Saved from dread death the greatest or the least
Who fell before the avenging Florentines.

   Alf. And did not even the arch-conspirator,
The Pope, die calmly in his bed?   Riario,
His nephew, sworn accomplice—doth he not
Live on in hoary age?   Thank Heaven, in Rome
We have no servile Florentines to mourn
A tyrant's death, or to avenge his fate ;
Nor need to meet in church or open street
The destined victim.   Gentler means are ours,
Such as thy skill may better find than mine.
Yet must the deed be done !

    Ver.   And done by me?

    Alf. By thee. (*Aside*) Be this thy fee for this brief hour
Of consultation.   [*Places a purse in his hand secretly.*

    Ver. (*aside*).   How can I accept,
Yet how refuse?   On either side is death !
I would seek leisure to reflect.   My veins
Feel as though fire, instead of mortal blood,
Were leaping through them, while my nerves are strained
As though the very cords of life would burst.
What have I said? what done?   I must away,
For now the Pontiff claims my services.
My work fulfilled, I will return to thee,

Lord Cardinal, and seek thy presence here.
(*Aside, and glancing doubtfully towards* Antonio) But let
   us talk alone !

Scene III.—*An apartment in the Vatican.* Laodamia
   and Violante (*entering together, the former, in great
   excitement, leaning on the latter*).

   Laod. Oh, I am wild.   My brain is whirling round ;
A tempest rages round me, and a gulf
Is opening at my feet.   Friend, sister, guide,
Oh, whither canst thou lead me ?
   Viol.   What new grief—
What greater grief than that we both have shared,
Hath fallen, can fall on us ?
   Laod.   As I passed through
Yon corridor, a messenger disguised
Placed this within my hand.   I know not why
I took it from him.   Could it be for me ?
I read one word, and then a blinding film
Came o'er my sight, for oh, that word was death !
Read it, and if thou canst, interpret it.
   Viol. Oh, calm thyself, and I will read.   Fear not
The wildest threat——
   Laod.   Read, read ; I *will* be calm !
   Viol. (*reads*). " If Don Alfonso's life is dear to thee,
Know that that life must perish in the storm
Which soon must burst o'er all his house and thine,
Unless thou save it.   Unto thee alone
This lot is given ; but thy protecting hand
Must seek its guidance from the hand that writes
These words of warning.   Meet me at the hour

Of midnight in the place where this is given thee.
Be cautious, for a double guard is placed
At the entrance of the corridor.   Fail not,
And all may yet be well.   But come alone ;
No witness must be near, or all is lost."

   Laod. Each word is as a dagger to my heart,
And strikes it in the dark.   What can I do ?
Were it not that the shadows of the past
Fall o'er my path, and gather in the distance,
Shrouding the sunset of our fading lives
Ere they go down in night, these words would read
But as a meaningless attempt to fright
A woman's heart.   But I have nought to fear,
And only one to love—and my poor life
Might well be given for his.

   Viol.   Alas ! my sister,
Such words are no mere threat.   In these dark walls,
Whose every stone might tell a tale of blood,
No heart is faithful, save the heart that bears
Deathless tradition of some ancient wrong
Or pent-up vengeance.   All—all else is false !
From other men, in other scenes, to obey
Such mandate would be madness ; but in Rome
To treat its warning with contempt might be
Even worse than madness—death !

   Laod.   I know not which
In this dread hour to choose—madness or death.
The one would veil us with unconsciousness
Of present ills, yet leave the comedy
Of life around us ; while the other brings
The welcome sentence of eternal sleep,
Which even the dream of life can vex no more.
But what must now be done ?

Viol.   'One only way
Reveals itself in this dark hour of need.
Thou must seek first Alfonso ; lay before him
This letter ; tell him that you have resolved
To face this nameless one, be he friend or foe ;
Then ask him, in some near recess concealed,
To guard thy life from danger.   At some sign
Agreed on, summon him to shield thy life
And guard his own, by this strange missive warned
Of coming danger.
    Laod.   Prudent is thy counsel,
And well and timely given.   But one more boon
I ask of thee—that thou companion me
On this dread errand ; aid me to explain
The hidden mystery of these threatening words,
Our duties and our fears.
    Viol.   I go with thee.
Haply we may o'ertake him as he passes
From the Consistory.
    Laod.   Lead—lead me to him ! [*Exeunt.*

SCENE IV.—*A corridor in the Vatican, dimly lighted.*

Enter LAODAMIA, *with a lamp.   A* Stranger, *concealed
in a mantle.*

    Laod. I know not whom in this dark midnight hour
And this strange place I meet.   Whoe'er thou art,
Stranger, I have trusted thee ; it is for thee
To prove I am not rash.   Tell me thy mission,
And let thy words be brief.
    Stranger.   My name, my office

Is not unknown to thee.   Of Don Alfonso
I am the secretary.
    Laod.   What ! Antonio ?
    Ant. (*throwing off his mantle*). The same !
    Laod.   Great God ! what mean these fearful words ?
Explain—interpret them !
    Ant.   My master's life
Hangs on a word—a breath.
    Laod.   What meanest thou ?
    Ant. He is engaged in a conspiracy
To slay the Sovereign Pontiff.
    Laod.   Never—never !
It cannot be.   Some wretch hath been suborned
To swear away his life.
    Ant.   That wretch is here,
If the possession of these fatal proofs
Brand him as traitor or as perjurer.
    Laod. Antonio, thou hast known him for long years ;
Thou knowest that every secret of his heart
Is writ upon his lips.   And darest thou say,
Impetuous, bold, and reckless though he be,
That he could harbour murderous plan or thought
Of secret treason ? e'er could lift his hand
Or aim a shaft against the Lord's anointed—
Even the great Pontiff whom his suffrage raised
To Peter's throne, his voice was first to acclaim ?
Go, tell thy tale to other ears than mine,
If this be all its burden.
    Ant.   Lady, hear me !
This paper, signed by Don Alfonso's hand,
Proves his dread guilt, and bears the signature
Of Don Vercelli.
    Laod.   What ! the Pope's physician ?

What name shall we hear next?   It may be, even
The Donna Maddalena's.   Merciful Heaven,
What life is safe in Rome?
    Ant.   Be calm; for else
These proofs of guilt, which but one word of thine
Might doom to swift destruction, must survive
To bring worse doom on him whom once thou lovedst.
    Laod. And still, still love; not now as once I loved,
Yet love as sister—bride of heaven and him!
But I have been too hasty.   Speak: what word
Of mine can save his life?
    Ant.   If but that word
Which once, with deeper than a sister's love,
Passed from thy heart to his, but now to him
May never more be uttered, could but fall
On mine, my life were blessed, his life secure!
    Laod. And darest thou, miscreant, claim my love as
        bribe
For Don Alfonso's life?   For that I would
Lay down my own.   But my first love and last
Is offered up to God; upon the shrine
Of his dear love who might not share it here
It rests, until it lives again in heaven,
Divorced no more for ever!
    Ant.   Yet bethink thee,
Long have I served thy house.   Alfonso owes
To me the power his name hath gained in Siena.
When he claimed thee as his affianced one,
I loved thee with a brother's love; when he
Could love thee but as brother, then my heart
Aspired to higher claim.   I dared to hope
That I might fill the place in thy fond heart
Which once was his.   I dared to think that I,

Whose tried fidelity was known and prized
By him thou lovedst the most, might find from thee
The glance of pity; that that glance might yet
Shine on, until it brightened into love.
Oh, say at least you hate me not, for then
You yet may pity me—may love me yet !

Laod. I never hated what I ne'er could love,
And never pitied what my inmost soul
Could only scorn.   Be this my last reply !

Ant. Lady, 'twere well that thou shouldst guard thy
speech.
The life thou lovest is in the hand of him
Whose love thou now hast spurned.   At least, his
vengeance
Thou darest not to despise.

Laod.   Vengeance belongs
To God alone.   My cause is in His hands ;
To Him I now commend it—and Alfonso's.

Ant. Oh, even in stern rejection beautiful,
I would that thou couldst hate me, if one spark
Of love could spring from the ashes of thy hate
To make me feel that thou rememberest me !
Let me, at least, adore thee ! [*Kneels and takes her hand.*

Laod. Ho !   Alfonso !

Alf. (appearing from a recess behind). Monster, fall
back ! kneel, if thou wilt, to God,
To seek His pardon for thy treacherous guilt.
Kneel to the master whom thou wouldst betray.
Kneel to the Pope who would reward thee better
Than this angelic one, whom heaven itself
Hath interposed to save !

Ant.   Lord Cardinal,
Thy life is in my hands.   This scroll attests
Thy treason——

Alf.   And thy shameless perfidy,
Or rather thine invention.
    Ant.   It was writ
At thy dictation, signed by Don Vercelli
And by thyself. Could proof be made more plain?
My part was only to record thy words
And be their faithful witness.
    Alf.   I defy thee
To prove the words thy lying pen hath writ.
Give me the scroll.
    Ant.   I give thee first my life.
Alf. I do accept thy gift; and thus the scroll
Shall perish with its witness at one blow!
    [*Seizes* ANTONIO. *They struggle, and the latter falls.*

Enter three Pontifical Guards.

Guard. Seize them! Within the Apostolic Palace
Conflict with arms is criminal.
    Alf.   I dare you
To touch me. As a prince of Holy Church,
None but an officer who bears a warrant
From the Pope himself can order mine arrest.
    Guard. Here is his order, duly signed and sealed,
And countersigned by the Master of the Palace.
                    [*Shows the order to* ALFONSO.
    Alf. It bears the signet of the Fisherman;
I must obey. But first let me conduct
This noble lady to her own apartment;
Then will we follow you.
    Guard.   Your Eminence
May trust to us as we to you. We do
Accept your pledge. From you, Messer Antonio,

We claim these papers, and must seal them here.
Their mysteries must be solved by keener wits
Than ours.   Firm hands and true and faithful hearts
Are all that we can claim.   God give thy soul
A good deliverance !
    Ant.   Lead on ; I follow.

END OF ACT IV.

ACT V.

SCENE I.—*The Consistory.* LEO X., *surrounded by the* Cardinals' Secretaries *and officials at a table in front of the Pope.**

Leo X. I have convoked you, venerable brothers,
Thus suddenly, through urgency of need
For your high counsel.   Treason walks abroad—
Not stealthily, as in the day when crime
Hid its dread aspect from the public gaze,
But with the proud disguise of patriotism ;
And those who stand the nearest to our throne
Are leagued against our life.   A murderous plot,
A foul conspiracy, whose roots are spread
Even in this Senate, hath revealed itself.
But the high Providence which in earlier day
Preserved for Rome the glory of the world
Hath succoured us, and saved this sacred throne,
Built on the ruins of its world-wide power.†
These papers, records of the hideous crime,
And tracking every tortuous path of guilt,

* The scene here presented is briefly described by Guicciar-dini, l. xiii.

† "Ma l'alta Provvidenza che con Scipio
   Difese a Roma la gloria del mondo
   Soccorrà tosto sì com' io concipio."
                    Dante, *Parad.*, c. xxvii. *v.* 61.

Have fallen into our hands.   The proofs are here ;
                              [*Produces the papers.*
And he who planned a guiltless Pontiff's death
Stands now before your eyes.

Enter ALFONSO, *between two* Pontifical Guards.

                              " How long wilt thou
Abuse our patience, and thy maddened rage
Elude our vigilance ?   *Quousque tandem ?*
Doth not the nightly watch in this our palace,
Fear of the people, concourse of good men,
This Senate's sacred scene, these hoary hairs,
Move thee to shame ? "   Alfonso, Cardinal,
Prince of the Church, and nephew of the friend
Whom most I love, whose care hath saved my life
From thy foul treason, I proclaim thee here
Traitor to God, and to His holy Church
An alien ; from the tree of life cut off,
As withered branch ; of all thy rights deprived ;
Disgraced, degraded, excommunicate !
    Alf. Your Holiness needs better proof than this
Of such unnatural guilt ; and I do here
Appeal as from the Pontiff ill-informed
To the same Pontiff better taught and schooled
To judge so hard a cause.*   Was it not I
Who raised thee to this pinnacle of power ?
And can mine be the traitor's arm that now
Would cast thee from it ?   Let my noble uncle
The Don Raffaello say, if say he dare,

---

* " Receptum est, a Sede.Apostolicâ appellari . . . ad eamdem
Sedem Apostolicam melius informatam " (" Van Espen," Part i. tit. ʌ.
ᴄ. ii. sect. 12).

That e'er I uttered threat or word of guilt
(I say not murder) in his hearing ; prove,
If prove he can, that writings forged and false,
Even though they feign my seal and signature,
Can be my work.   Is such guilt probable ?
Is it even possible, as against the prince
Who owes to me his throne—the power to bless
And heal with mercy, or with curse to blast
As it would blast me now.   The wretch who builds
His sordid fortune on his master's loss
Is not the man who boldly pleads his cause
Before your Holiness, nor fears to meet
The traitor who would rise but by his fall.
    Leo X. I dare not trust myself to hear thee farther,
Lest the weak heart of him who loved thee once
Should stay the hand of justice.   Leave our presence,
And we will weigh your words and these dread proofs
In even balance.   Guards, remove your prisoner !
                    [*Exeunt* Guards *with* Alfonso.
To sift this evidence with legal skill,
By the stern rules of our Pontifical law,
Befits not our high office.   We remit
The cause, with all its facts and incidents,
To our tried prefect, Mario Perusco,*
Chief judge of all our causes criminal,
On whose report, maturely weighed, must rest
The changeless judgment of this Holy See.   [*Pauses.*
But now a yet more painful task remains.
Not only the young members of our Senate
Are leagued against us, but the ancient men,
The elders of our Israel, princes of

* This reference of the case to a civil judge provoked the protest
of the Spanish ambassador in the interests of the foreign Cardinals.

This holy Congregation.   This dread paper
Records their names.   I dare not trust mine eye
To scan them, or my lips to utter them ;
I close in grief the page.   But in the name
Of God and Holy Church, we summon all
Who may be present here, and cite all those
Who from this high Consistory are absent,
If they are conscious of this hidden crime,
And knowing it, concealed its treason-guilt,
To kneel before us, and repentant claim
Our high indulgence, and impunity
From the dread penalty that falls on those
Who fail to guard the Pontiff's sacred life.   [*Pauses.*
And now, on pain of excommunication,
We do enjoin strict silence for a space,
That ye may judge your hearts and purge yourselves
From this dark crime.   Now only is the time
Accepted ; now the day of your salvation.

       [*A solemn silence ensues, in the midst of which*
          Cardinal Riario *comes forward and kneels*
          before the Pope.

  Ria. First among those who heard the direful threats
Uttered by Don Alfonso, and who failed
Through fear their guilty purpose to disclose,
I kneel before your Holiness, and pray
Your mercy for my frailty.   Age and grief,
Twin guides which help me onward to the grave,
Have made my strength to fail me.   They alone
Must plead for me, and cover my great guilt !

  Leo X. (*raising him*).   I do forgive thee ! Go, and sin
      no more ;
Thy late confession not too late atones
For silence which would else be base connivance.

          [Cardinal Soderini *kneels before the* Pope.

What ! Soderini ? kinsman * Florentine !
Alas ! our foes are those of our own household.
Whom can we trust ?

 Sod.   Before your Holiness
I kneel to claim the mercy thou hast granted
To Don Riario. We were one, alas !
In knowledge of these threats, but fear of death
Held back the power of speech. Yet had we known
That threats had ripened into plans of guilt,
Our utterance had returned.

 Leo X.   'Tis well for thee
That it returns this day. Thou art forgiven !
But thou, Lord Cardinal Bandinello Saulio,
Involved more deeply in this dark design,
Must wait the judgment of thy brethren, ere
We can include thee in this welcome word
Of high absolving grace. We meet to-morrow
In fullest senate, and thus give thee time
To perfect thy defence. But for to-day
Our task is done. Let the Prothonotary
Declare this high Consistory dissolved.

   Scene II.—*The prison.* Alfonso ; Laodamia.

 Laod. Oh that my deathless love
Could be the ransom of thy life, my tears
Blot out the writing of thy guilt ! Alas !
They have but writ thy sentence. But for me,
Antonio might have yielded up the proofs

---

 * The mother of Soderini was Dianora Tornabuona, the near
relation (probably sister) of the famous Lucrezia Tornabuona, the
grandmother of Leo X.

Of that dark interview.   I sought to shield,
But I have pierced thee; strove to save from death,
But I have slain thee.

     Alf.   Speak !   What meanest thou ?

     Laod. Had I but met that monster's base advance
With prudent self-control, and gained from him
That fatal scroll, I might have saved thy life.
I was too rash, too proud ; I could not bear
To hear him speak of me as one he loved.
I could have been his slave to save thy life,
But never loved another life than thine.

     Alf. Oh, goad me not to madness.   Even the thought
Of that dark midnight hour which saw him kneel
Before thee is a dagger to my soul,
Sharper than traitor's knife or Pope's revenge.

     Laod. Yet was the charge he laid against thee keener
Than murderer's blade, direr than papal curse.
Alfonso, tell me that that roll was forged—
That those dread papers were false witnesses
Suborned by him !

     Alf.   His treason were the same,
If they were false or true.

     Laod.   Oh, leave me not
That poor alternative.   Say they were false,
And let me keep my faith.

     Alf.   'Twere hard indeed
To tell thee what they were, for truth is oft
So mixed with falsehood that the keenest wit
Might scarce divide them.   It may be that much
Was writ that I spake lightly, much set down
That I had never said.

     Laod.   Yet how canst thou
Explain that fatal compact, pledging thee

To give reward to him whose traitorous hand
Fulfilled some unnamed deed?
  Alf.   Such unnamed deeds
Live only in the thoughts of him whose tongue
Can give them place and name. Let the vile slaves
Who hover round the Court interpret them.
  Laod. Canst thou thus tamper with thy life, and rack
With doubts even worse than death this martyred love?
Say—art thou guilty? art thou innocent?
There is no middle course. I seem to stand
As in the purging flames ; I wait for thee
To pray me out of fires, oh, worse than those
Of guilt unshriven.
  Alf.   Oh, loved one, could my cause
Be tried by thee, thy true unswerving faith
Would prove me innocent. For if to plan
A tyrant's death were crime, then war itself,
Even for our holiest rights or bitterest wrongs,
Would be but murder, wholesale, manifold,
Which yet men crown with glory.
  Laod.   Oh, Alfonso,
Thy passion wrongs thine heart ; the insatiate lust
For vengeance tramples out each holier thought.
It was not thus thou spakest when this fond heart
Owned thee its lord ; it was not thus thou spakest
When to a higher life this widowed love
Surrendered thee. I feared not for thee then ;
But now, how can I fear not? Leave, oh, leave me
The creed of my first love—the faith that thou,
Even 'neath the cloud which veils thy soul from mine,
Art still the being that I loved at first,
And, ah ! must love for ever. If thou art guilty,
May God forgive thee ! We are guilty all ;

Yet will I still believe thine innocence,
And pray that my first faith may be my last.
There are some crimes which even to hardened guilt
Can be scarce possible, and such is that
Which they have laid on thee.

  Alf.   I grudge thee not
That fond belief; and if thy love distrust
My guilt, and can survive the traitor's fate
Which now o'erhangs me, I shall rest in peace,
And shall not die unblest.

  Laod.   O faith! O hope!
How weak are ye to struggle with the doubts,
The fears that rack my soul! Yet bear me onward,
And Thou, the Lord of all, supremely throned
O'er the wild conflicts of this lower world,
Teach my unconquered heart to live, to die
In the true faith that he I loved on earth
Is innocent—to write that word of faith
Even upon my grave.

  Alf.   Oh, saintly one,
I loved thee once, but now my love is changed
To adoration. If I may not live
In heaven with thee, I yet will worship thee,
And thou wilt light for me that darkening gulf
From which I may not rise. Farewell for ever!

SCENE III.—*The Apartments of* DONNA MADDALENA *in
the Vatican.* LAODAMIA; MADDALENA.

  Laod. Oh, Donna Maddalena, thy young heart,
Though it may ne'er have felt the stroke of grief,
Can feel the touch of pity.

Mad.   What new sorrow,
Poor child, hath fallen on thee?
    Laod.   Alas! the doom
Which on Alfonso falls, with heavier weight
Must fall on me.
    Mad.   My child, what meanest thou?
    Laod. I was betrothed to him in earliest years.
I loved him; in dark hour, by base intrigue,
He was snatched from me. Don Borghese feared
His rivalry in Siena, and Pandolfo
Leagued with Riario to persuade the Pope
To make him Cardinal, to wean him from
His early love by proud ambition's lust.
Forced by my sire and them, I yielded him—
Crushed the dear memories of a loving life
Like springtide flowers beneath my feet, and then
Sprang up along my path the poisonous weeds
Of bitter grief to bear the fruits of death.
Oh, Maddalena, if thou e'er hast known
The dearth of loneliness, the joys of love,
The pang of parting even for brief days
From one thou lovest, think how terrible
'Twould be to part for ever, and to see
The loved one pass through torments worse than death
Into the unseen world, before whose void
Even faith is struck with palsy of despair,
And prayer shrinks trembling. Yet such grief is mine!
And though, through cruel fate, a sister's lot
Is all I now can claim, the martyrdom
Of suffering love, the sacrifice of self,
That he might live a higher life than mine,
While I might gaze on him as from afar,
Till we can claim an angel's ministry,

Divorced no more—this, this hath raised my soul
Above the world, the grave, and death itself;
And now even this must fail me, and the day
Of my soul's famine dawn!

  Mad.   Poor victim of
A love that hath beguiled and must consume thee,
How can I help thee? Even now 'tis said
That the dread sentence of a parricide
Hath been pronounced on him thy love might once
Have raised to saintly life. Yet now that justice
Hath had her sway, mercy may interpose
And stay the blow, though not arrest the sentence.
But work like this brooks not an hour's delay.
We must seek audience of the Pope; there plead—
Thou with the eloquence of suffering love,
Myself with all a woman's sympathy—
For him, for thee. May Heaven with blest success
Crown our importunate prayers!

  Laod.   And thy dear love
With life of peace and diadem of glory!   [*Exeunt.*

SCENE IV.—*The Pope's private apartments in the Vatican.*
  LEO X.; CARDINAL CORNELIO.

  Cor. I do conjure your Holiness to pause
In this dread business. Lend not ready ear
To Don Raffaello. For the coveted prize
Of Siena's lordship he would hold but cheap
The lives of all his race. Oh, suffer not
The sacred purple to be stained with blood,
A Cardinal to be tortured as a slave.
Since Urban's reign of terror and of guilt,

When thrilling cries of tortured Cardinals
Ascended to high heaven, such sickening sight
Hath ne'er in Rome been witnessed.*   Is it yet
Too late to stay thine hand?

Leo X.   I know not whether
This strongest remedy for stubborn guilt
Hath been resorted to.   I cannot stay
The march of justice, or prescribe its course.
When the stern rule of the Pontifical law
Hath been enforced, mercy may claim its due,
But not till then.

Cor.   Yet what if (as 'tis said)
He hath confessed his guilt?

Leo X.   'Tis not enough:
He must denounce his fell accomplices.
His guilt stands forth by clearest evidence;
Theirs must be proved by him.

Cor.   Oh, hadst thou been
With us in yonder judgment-hall to see
The form of Don Alfonso, standing forth
In all its youthful beauty, moved with grief
That death, and such a death, so soon would mar
So fair a life, thine inmost soul, like ours,
Had melted into pity, longed to hear
Some gentler sentence.   For when Don Rinaldo
Rose, at the judges' stern behest, to read
Their finding and decree, a thrill of grief
Passed through the crowd, so saddening and so deep

* The horrible cruelties of Urban VI. to the captive Cardinals,
whom he dragged about with him, even ordering the murder of one
of them on the road, are detailed by his secretary Theodoricus à
Niem, an eye-witness, in the first book of his history of the great
schism.

That I was fain to weep, and dared not lift
Mine eyes to gaze around me.   Then there fell
Upon mine ear the voice of that grave man
In race the kinsman, and in love the sire
Of the rash youth whose doom inflexible,
In cruel mockery of his grief, he was
Constrained to read—the sentence of sure death
Not less to her whose love was his sole bliss,
Than to Alfonso, yea, and to himself.
Oh, as each accent trembled into life,
Or, choked by strong emotion, died away
Upon the burdened air, what tongue might tell
The grief that filled our breasts !

    Leo X. :   Thou feelest, methinks,
Less for the victim of so great a crime
Than for its agent—like the king of old
Who mourned for Absalom.   If he but lived,
And all our lives had perished through his guilt,
It would have pleased thee well.

    Cor.   Thou dost misjudge
The motive of my words.   They but invoke
Thy mercy for the criminal ; the crime
Who can extenuate ?

               Enter a Messenger.

    Mess.   Your Holiness
Is importuned by the Donna Maddalena
To give your gracious audience to herself
And to a suppliant friend.

    Leo X.   My sister needs ·
No importunity to urge her suit ;
Tell her we welcome her.   [*Exit* CORNELIO.

Enter MADDALENA *with* LAODAMIA.

Mad. My brother, raised to this high pinnacle
Of earthly greatness and of heavenly power,
We need to feel with tenderer care and love
For those who, like the martyred saints of old,
Are children of the sorrows of the cross ;
And this sad daughter of our faith and race
Is bent down to the earth by load of grief
So heavy, that thy heart may well be moved
With pity for her state.   Laodamia,
Approach and claim a father's love for him
Who might have borne for thee a husband's name.
   Laod. (*kneeling before the Pope*). I cannot speak ; my
      tears must be my prayers.
Their source thou know'st too well.
   Leo X. (*raising her up*).   Alas ! poor child,
Thou hast loved, and, in blind ignorance of his
      guilt,
Hast loved a parricide.
   Laod.   And love him still,
Because I feel, I know that, if not free
From guilt, he hath by treacherous guides been led
To the dread brink of this dark infamy,
And that the heart that loves must yet repent.
But as his sentence hath been now decreed
And justice had her reign, it is for thee,
Of God's eternal mercy minister,
To say with thy Great Master, "Go, my son,
And sin no more ! " Oh, what a fount of love
Would be unsealed within Alfonso's heart
By word like this ! The purple then would be
Sprinkled with tears of grateful love, not stained

With blood, which no repentant tears might else
Wipe from the great remembrance book of God.

    Mad. What word of mine can add to this great
        plea
Of faith, of love, from breaking heart sent forth?
Thou know'st, my brother, to Francesco Cibo
I am betrothed. Thy love hath promised me
A fitting dowry. Oh, be this thy gift—
If not to pardon, at the least to save
Alfonso from the doom of fearful death!

    Leo X. I dare not promise unconditioned mercy
In case like this. Murder might else stalk forth,
And hand in hand with sacrilege invade
Our homes, and make our holiest things a prey.
Such pardon needs securities. Our life
Is menaced here in Rome, our rule in Siena.
If but Alfonso yield himself to us,
And pledge allegiance to the Don Raffaello,
Renounce his claims, denounce the accomplices
In this great treason, we might take his case
Into our high consideration; change
His fearful penalty to lighter doom.

    Laod. I cannot barter with thee for a life
As though it were mere merchandise. To him
Pardon on terms like these were worse than death,
And life a brand of shame.

    Mad.   My child, forbear
From such dread utterance.

    Laod.   '   Oh, Maddalena,
Forgive me! And forgive me, Holy Father!
I minded not that thou art God's high priest,
Else would those words which pierced my heart have
        fallen

As on the desert air, where no response
But their own echo could have reached thine ear.
  Leo X. My sister, it were useless to prolong
This scene of misery.   In thy loving care
We leave this suppliant. , Let her prove her love
To him whose innocence, with childlike faith
And childish petulance, she urges still,
By leading him to own his guilt, denounce
The partners of his crime, renounce his claims
On Siena, and without reserve submit
His cause to me.   I *might* be merciful,
But I *must* first be just.

Scene V.—*The prison.*   Laodamia ; Alfonso.

  Laod. All, all hath failed !   The gentle Maddalena,
Angel of light in these dark halls of death,
Brought me before the Pope ; appealed for thee,
For me, with all the artless eloquence
Of a pure life, a heart which hath not yet
Unlearned the tenderness of woman's love,
Though she ne'er knew its grief.
  Alf.   And what said he,
The fabled successor of saints and martyrs,
Who builds their tombs but to allow the deeds
Of those who slew them ?
  Laod.   Few and cold his words,
Worthy of all his race.   Like broker, sworn
To appraise the few last days of thy poor life,
He named his price—laid down conditions.
Had I come there with gold like old Riario,
Or ample lands, I might perchance have bought

Oblivion for thy guilt, as he for his.*

Alf. And what were his conditions?

Laod.   To denounce
The partners of thy crime, renounce thy claims
On Siena, and give fealty to Raffaello;
Then might he yet give ear unto my prayer
And save thy life.

Alf.   I will not ask what then
Thou saidst. My more than life was in thy hands,
And thou, the angel of our name and race,
Couldst not betray it. But my time is short.
My days are numbered, and this meeting hour
Is measured out by seconds. See, the sand
Is running low.

Laod.   Oh, Don Alfonso, say
But one, one word—that thou art innocent,
Or, if not innocent, repentant. Leave
This last best heritage to stay my heart
And be its bread of life when thou art gone.
Then will I wear away this life of pain
In importunity of prayer and deeds
Of mercy, and will build again for thee
The altar of my love. Said I "again"?
It stands; no human hand can cast it down,
No papal curse can make it desecrate.
Give me, then, this last pledge of constant love,
Friend—brother—guide—I dare not call thee more—
Betrothed and parted—parting now for ever!

                                 [*Falls on his neck.*

---

* Riario ransomed his life for the enormous sum of 100,000 golden crowns. Soderini gave 10,000 for his life, while Saulio was killed "with a slow poison" (see Palatius in his life of Leo X., who quotes Folieta; "Elogia Clariss. Ligurum ").

Alf. Oh, saint of God, too sacred for the love
Of mortal stained with guilt and doomed to pay
The price of maddening wrath, I have nought to leave
Save the eternal memory of a love
That must live on where'er our lot may be,
And through thy prayers may live with thine in
        bliss.
I *do* repent—I would that I could say
Believe and hope.   Thy prayers must gain for me
The faith I lost too soon, the hope that sinks
On the dark horizon of a life of guilt.

Laod. Yet thou art penitent, and thy dear love
Is stainless; how then can I deem thee false
To him who is the bond of all our loves,
Uniting all in Christ?   A wondrous dream
Of joy comes o'er me.   These grim walls are changed
To the fair palace where, in earlier days,
We spake of love—the cradle of our race.
I see the orange-groves where once we walked,
And watched the domes of Siena as they met
The rising sun, or basked in the long sunset.
Oh, they were days of bliss; and they return
To gaze on us as from a distant world,
And mock the ruins of our outraged love !
Alfonso, say, oh, say thy heart is true—
That those blest days gave not false prophecy.
Say that thou lovest me still.   Yet rather say
That thou art innocent.   For that one word
I would give up—not life, for life to me
Is living death; but more, far more—thy love !

Alf. Yet have we lived to prove that all is false
Save that undying love ; and can my guilt
Be true where all is false ?   Thy truth alone,

Thy pitying glance, reminds me there is yet
A pardoning God.
   Laod.   Oh, be His pardon thine,
And mine to pray for it, till prayer no more
Can rise from this lone heart.   Oh, God ! to part
So soon ! to die so young !   Farewell, farewell !
   Alf. Yet not for ever ; for my life of guilt
Shall cleave to thee, and thou wilt cleave to Him
From whom no curse of Pope or prince on earth
Can ever rend thee !   (*Looks at the hour-glass.*)   But the
       hour hath come !
The guard is at the door.

Enter a Guard.

   Guard.   Most noble lady,
The hour of interview is o'er.
   Laod.   Great God,
Be with him to the last.   I may not be.
Farewell, farewell ! and be thy words mine own—
" Yet not for ever ! "   [*Exeunt.*

SCENE VI.—*A gallery adjoining the prison, lit with a
    faint lamp.* LAODAMIA, *entering it, meets* ORLANDO,
    formerly in the service of ALFONSO.

   Laod. Orlando, is it thou ?   By what strange chance
Hath it befallen thee to keep watch and ward
Over thy master's son ?
   Orl.   By the same chance
Which made me first his slave.

Laod.   Nay, answer kindly.
The lord Pandolfo was thy faithful friend ;
He saved thy life from pirates, who had doomed
To death their captives, when with mightier arm
He rescued thee.

Orl.   To doom that life to slavery ;
Though in these veins the holy Prophet's blood
Flows pure and clear, even as through dark ravine
The mountain torrent.

Laod.   Yet thou owest thy life
To him, and but for him its current now
Would be choked up in death.

Orl.   'Twere better far
To choke it at its source, than make its stream
Stagnant and thick in the polluted air
Of Rome or Siena.

Laod.   Oh, let former wrongs
Be now forgotten.   Think of him who once
Was thy fond playmate, loved thee, followed thee,
Hung breathlessly upon thy wondrous tales
Of Moorish life, of wild and valiant deeds
Wrought by thy kinsmen.   He could wrong thee not ;
And if *he* lives, thy life, thy freedom too,
Shall live with his.

Orl.   Lady, 'twere doubtful gain
To save a traitor.   He who breaks his faith
May never mend it ; and that faith was pledged
To him whom he believes in as his prophet,
His great high priest.

Laod.   Why call Alfonso traitor
On a mere traitor's word ?   To thee, at least,
He hath been faithful.   Oh, condemn him not ;
But soothe for him his dread captivity

With the blest thought that one who knew him first
Dares trust him to the end.
  Orl.   And could I trust him
When to his brother he was faithless found?
Could he who had betrayed his master prove
True to a slave like me?
  Laod.   Oh, good Orlando,
I thought not this of thee. Thy race is famed
For faith unwavering and invincible,
For love forsaking not when all forsake.
Oh, I would here invoke it—claim at least
Thy pity for his fate whom once thou lovedst.
Thou canst not hate him now. [ORLANDO *passes on.*
  Laod. Oh, whither can I turn in this dark maze
Of cruelty and wrong? I have no guide,
And wander on companionless. In vain
I ask my way; no human tongue replies.
The voices of the howling wilderness
Bring back my prayers upon my breaking heart !
Oh, if Alfonso could but say that word,
" I am innocent !" if I could find but one
To disbelieve his guilt, but one to cast
His mite of faith into the treasury
Of this fond heart which loved and loves him still !
If I could wake one kindly thought in those
Who envied once, and well might pity now !
But who is this approaching?

     Enter VIOLANTE.

         Violante?
Oh, wherefore here? For me this scene of death
Seems like a birthplace. But for thee?

Viol.   My sister,
My birthplace still is thine; for kindred souls
Are born together, must together bear
The yoke of life, and then together die.
But I must lead thee hence.   Thy heart-rent sire
. Is wandering frantic, wildly pacing on
Through this vast maze of halls and corridors,
Uttering thy name to every passing breeze
Which but returns his moan.   Oh, leave with me
This charnel-house.   Return to the upper air
From this dark stifling gloom.
  Laod.   I cannot move.
My heart is chained, my limbs are paralyzed;
The chill of death comes o'er me.   Do I live,
Or is even life a dream?
  Viol.   '   Oh, lean on me,
And I will lean on God.   He bears our cross
Who friendless bare His own.
  Laod.   I cannot move.
I dread me that his hour of doom is nigh,
And mine must strike with his !   If he lives still,
Here still I live with him ; if here he dies,
I die.   Thou wilt not bid me to live on
When my poor heart is dead.
  Viol.   My child, be calm.
Live for the sire who still must claim thy love ;
Live even for me.   This prison air hath chilled
Thy very life-blood.   Come, oh, come with me.
  Laod. Nay, touch me not.   Fear not that I shall
   .faint ;
I feel an arm I never felt before
Sustaining me.   Great God, what do I hear?
It is Alfonso's voice !

Viol.   'Tis but the wind
Howling along the corridor.
      Laod.   Nay, nay;
It is his voice. It is a shriek of anguish.
Canst thou deceive me? Know I not his voice?
There, there; dost hear it now?
      Viol.   I hear strange sounds,
As of wild men in conflict. 'Tis perchance
Some prison orgy. Every day we hear
Such strifes as these in the streets, and why not here?
      Laod. Oh, trifle not with such a grief as mine.
Hark ! 'tis his voice again, and now a cry
As of the hideous Moor exulting o'er
His unarmed victim,* and a sound I hear
As of two struggling men. God give him strength !
There is a heavy fall, a dying groan.
It is Alfonso's !
      Viol.   Child, it is thy dream.
Oh, wake to life. Rinaldo ! Lord of heaven,
Oh, bring him quickly ! Thine be all the praise,
He comes !

              Enter RINALDO, *conducted by a* Guard.

      Rin. Last treasure of this bursting heart,
Oh, let me lead thee hence. Come, come with me,
Lest this dank air put out the only light
Which guides me to the grave.
      Laod.   My sire ! my life !
My prayer is answered. 'Twas that thou mightst come.
                          [RINALDO *takes her hand.*

      * "In profundum, obtorto collo, perductus, eodem die ferro per
cussus vitam finiit, cum carnifice luctando Orlando Æthiope'
(Palatii, "Fasti Card.").

No, not to lead me hence, but here to take
My last, last breath ; to witness that my love
Lives in the darkness of this prison-house,
Lives in the night of death.   The blow that fell
Upon Alfonso, with yet surer aim
Hath fallen on me.   My life of life is dead,
And the poor life which gave it outward form
Sinks with it to the grave.   And thou, my sire,
Wilt lay that life with his.   Even if he's doomed
To have the burial of a parricide,
Wound up in sackcloth shroud, and cast into
The Tiber, whose dull waves tell silently
Of ruined lives, of memories buried deep,
Of all the guilt and grief which these dark walls
Have witnessed, and shall witness yet to heaven
When earth no more can cover up her slain —
If such a grave be his, oh, let me share it,
And I shall rise with him to plead the ills,
The cruel wrongs which turned a loving life
Into a life of madness.   But my strength
Is failing ; let me lean upon thy breast—
There sleep my life away.
 Rin.   Sleep there, my child ;
Yet sleep to wake again.   This loving breast
Pillowed thine infancy.   Oh, be thy sleep
As sweet as it was then, thy waking smile
As bright.   But thou art cold !
 Viol. (placing her hand on her forehead).   Oh, Don
  Rinaldo,
She sleeps, but ne'er to wake.   She seemed to hear,
Or heard (God only knows), the stroke of death
Fall on the form she loved, and as it fell
It was her death-stroke too.   The higher life

            G

Struggled in vain to quell the earlier love,
Pure as itself, and in the fearful strife
Her soul was borne to God.

Rin.   And I have been
The priest of that dread sacrifice ! 'Twas I
Who changed a wife's into a sister's love,
And hid the earlier flame I could not quench,
And it hath now consumed her.

Viol.   Oh, forbear
To linger on the past.   'Tis past to her ;
Oh, be it past to us.

Rin.   Yet must I close
Those loving eyes, feel if that heart still beats.
I feel it.   Feel it with me, Violante,
And tell me it still beats.

Viol.   'Tis but the throb
Of thy poor feverish hand.   Alas ! her heart
Can beat no more for ever.   Bear us hence,
Kind guards, and be her martyred form embalmed
In prayers and tears, preventing that glad day
When gain of heaven shall every loss restore,
And earth-wronged soul can suffer wrong no more.

THE END.

PRINTED BY WILLIAM CLOWES AND SONS, LIMITED, LONDON AND BECCLES.